THE LANGUAGE OF LIGHT

A NOVEL

KATHLEEN BRADY

Bywater
BOOKS

2022

Bywater Books

Copyright © 2022 Kathleen Brady

Print ISBN: 978-1-61294-223-0

Bywater Books First Edition: February 2022

Printed in the United States of America on acid-free paper.

Cover design: TreeHouse Studio

Bywater Books
PO Box 3671
Ann Arbor MI 48106-3671

www.bywaterbooks.com

To Happy Elliot and Helen Rifkin, because you were.
To Sydney Eaker, because you are.

BUILDING EIGHT

八娄

It was a generous midnight. The lighting in the Beijing airport had an easy dim, like the wattage of a back porch light left on for a late arrival.

The military guards, in droopy green uniforms cinched tightly at the waist with brown plastic belts, looked as though they had been awakened just before our aircraft's landing and were eager to resume their naps. When a soldier noticed that I saw him, he quickly slipped into the half-lit shadows. The baggage carousel seemed to have been constructed from recycled pallet lumber, and it jerked and groaned into its spin. But soon enough my two bags slid down to my eager hands.

I hailed a taxi and handed the driver the address of the Institute that my Chinese teacher in America had written down for me. The cabbie looked at the note, popped the trunk, and put my bags into the car. When he got back behind the wheel, I caught his glance in the rearview mirror as he started the car. Looking quickly away he put the car into gear and we were off. I clutched my purse to my chest like armor as trucks and buses

1

approached us with their headlights dark, flicking them on and off just as they passed during the one-hour ride.

As we sped along the dark road I thought of my friends, Eloise, Theresa, and Wendy, back in Los Angeles. They said I was nuts to come to Beijing to learn Mandarin, that I was running away from a broken heart, but they had still taken me out to a lavish breakfast and driven me to the airport for the thirteen-hour flight. When we got to the gate there were hugs and tears and kisses. I had promised to write, but now I wasn't so sure. I was traveling to my future and they were already a part of my past.

The taxi driver stopped in front of Building Eight at the Language Institute and I dragged my two suitcases inside, unintentionally waking up the doorkeeper, the woman responsible for screening visitors to the building. She swung open the door of her room with a bang.

"I am just here from America. Do you know where I should go now?"

"Speak Chinese!" she fog-horned.

I flattened against the wall as she hustled past me and up a staircase, and I was glad she was gone. I hesitated to speak the Chinese I knew because my teachers in America were from Taiwan and I had their Southern accent; I was skittish about political overtones.

A few minutes later a sleepy woman in a blue cotton dress came down the stairs. Her dress had hitched up on the left side and she finished pulling it down as she walked to me and extended her hand. Her braids were frayed and a long sleep wrinkle creased her left cheek.

"My name is Ming. I will take you to a room. Anything you touch you must bring with you tomorrow when we give your room, for sanitary."

"You speak English. Oh I am so happy to meet you. My name is Louise."

"I welcome you," she said, shaking my hand. "You must always try to speak Chinese. I will show you to a room just to sleep. You can eat in the morning at eight o'clock when the dining hall opens."

She left me in a room that was, by my measure, fifteen by twenty-five feet. The room, like Beijing, smelled like jasmine and mothballs, a curious blend that was oddly pleasant and singular. Each side of the room had a twin bed, a desk and a chair, a bookshelf, and a wardrobe. The floor was cement, and the walls were a dusty blue. There were no decorations anywhere, no curtains, no rugs; nothing was soft except, I hoped, the bed.

I turned off the overhead fluorescent light and opened the windows. I tested the mattress; it was like a futon with some springiness, and maybe a foot wider than the twin size I was used to. The pillow was baffling. It was heavy and seemed to be filled with tiny pebbles. There was just enough light from the outside lamps that I could find some toilet paper in my purse. I remembered from my tourist trip here in 1980 that you always carried your own toilet paper. I went into the communal bathroom and chose a stall. There it was, that ubiquitous squat toilet. It looked like a urinal lying on its back. I knew I would lose my balance if I tried to squat forward, so I used the toilet backwards and hung onto the pipes. I turned a four-inch red faucet handle to flush, and then turned it off. Would I ever get used to this?

I got into bed. Thankfully, it was comfortable. As I stretched out, I felt an unexpected longing. *Julia*. We had been together for nearly five years when she announced she was leaving to be with my best friend. It had been about a year since I last saw her, but whenever I cooked a meal for friends, read the Sunday newspaper, or took a walk on the beach, I remembered how we used to do those things together. Julia's desertion was especially painful when I connected it to my mother abandoning me at a boarding school. My ache for Julia made me angry and sad, and my tears rolled onto the peculiar pillow. I swore again to never love anyone so deeply.

Loudspeakers woke me up at 6 a.m. Except for counting—*yi, er, san,* or one, two, three—I couldn't understand what was announced, so I dismissed it as the school's news bulletins. I took in the daylight dimensions of the room. It was third world, spare, and utilitarian. I was hungry but it was too early for the dining hall, so I decided to take a walk and see what the campus looked like.

I pushed open two big front doors and there, just past the steps, was the woman I had met the night before. She was talking with several African students whose clothing was a spill of colors. And when they moved on, she turned and saw me.

"Louise, walk with me until the dining hall opens. I will show you around. Your responsible teacher wants to meet you this afternoon at two o'clock. I will show you the way to his office."

On our right were two bike racks with a jumble of black bicycles. We walked along in silence for a few minutes, following a low, well-tended hedge.

"How come that woman went to get you last night? Do you have a job here?"

"I am like your teacher, Su. I am responsible for Thai, Norwegian and Icelandic students. I have fifteen students. Teacher Su has just four students because Americans are more complicated. There are many more details between our governments since our relations are still new. Zhang came to me because I can speak English. I have a room in Building Eight for this reason. Otherwise, I would share a room with four others in a teachers' building."

The hedge continued on our right. On the left, a Chinese flag: red, with its five bright yellow stars, hung limply, marking the start of two basketball courts and then three tennis courts. The nets sagged and chunks of asphalt were missing where the

4

line markers would be. Off in the distance was a soccer pitch that might have had some grass, but looked to be mostly gray dirt. Nearby there was a huge red sign with very large black characters proclaiming something.

"What does that sign over there say?"

"Always do your best," she answered.

Six months later, I learned that she had given me the essentially correct translation. What she left out was the political encouragement to learn from the workers, soldiers and peasants.

Suddenly a colossal chorus of clicks and buzzes began, like six thousand decks of cards being shuffled all at once.

"What's that noise?"

"They are bugs, I think *cicadas* in English. They won't hurt you. Children like to catch them and put them into little bamboo cages. Some people eat them."

Really, I thought, *is my life here going to be a survival course? Eat bugs? No way.*

The August morning got hotter, muggier. The green hedge ended at a circular area ringed by glass-enclosed billboards and benches set below them. It was a relief to finally walk in the shade of weeping willow trees. The air smelled pleasant and I wasn't sure if it was my guide or the red and blue flowers growing near the billboards. We sat down on a bench and she handed me an extra handkerchief to wipe my sweating face. The billboards, she explained, were showcases where the teachers put up their students' calligraphy each month for a competition. First prize was a coveted cotton towel.

"See that window on the third floor, the second one from this corner?" she said, leaning a little closer to me so that I could track her pointing. "That is Teacher Su's office. If you want to visit other cities, he will tell you how to get a travel permit. This afternoon he will give you a permission note to buy a bicycle. I will go with you to pick a good bicycle if you want," she said flicking her left braid over her shoulder, offering a shy half smile.

5

I was realizing that she had just flirted with me when the cicadas started up again. I had to lean in a little closer to hear her. It was she and not the flowers that smelled so faintly sweet. I lingered for a full moment in that closeness to her. This was the first time I had ever heard these deafening and intriguing bugs. For a speedy moment I wondered what they looked like and how they might taste.

"What's a good brand of bike to buy?" I asked moving a little away from her.

"I have the 'Flying Pigeon.' It is a strong bike and is easy for fix. Don't worry if you break down. You are a foreigner, and people will stop to help you."

"Does my blonde hair make me special," I asked, "or is it because I'm so cute?"

I had just flirted back with her. What the hell was I doing?

Her swift look of surprise spread to a faint smile, and she laughed. "It is because you are a guest in China and people will always be polite and helpful." In a short time I would learn that "guest" would have several other meanings.

"It is time for the dining hall to open. I will walk you. We have students from sixty-four countries, so life can be very interesting. Go first to the ticket desk. You will need a ticket for the food. Tell him that you have just arrived and he will give you one. After you see Teacher Su, you can buy more tickets and return the one he gives you this morning."

She started to walk away and then turned back to me. "After breakfast go to Zhang, you know her from last night, then go to the room where you slept. Wait for me. Then we will help you move your things."

My goodness, she had an attractive way about her. Her English was charming; so was the way she flirted. Her coloring was a bit darker than most Chinese women, and she had a hint of swagger. I liked her curves, and the way she slipped into laughter. I hoped we could be friends.

6

The dining hall was crowded and loud. Students were laughing, and benches and stools scraped the cement floor. I stared at a group of African women dressed in the most stunning clothing I had ever seen: reds and yellows and greens that exploded with brilliance. In a quick glance I spotted Arab students in burnooses, a few women wearing the hijab, and some French-speaking women dressed in shorts and halter tops.

A pantomime exchange got me a meal ticket from the man at the desk, and I stood in the middle of the dining hall wondering what the next step was. I followed a few folks over to a four-foot tall glass display case made of cheap, wavy green glass. The dishes were numbered one through six. I decided on #6: a bowl of rice, two fried eggs and a bun. Beyond the case was a series of serving windows and I stood in the one that had the shortest line. But when I got to the front, I learned that the plate numbers matched the window numbers, and I was not at window 6. I lined up again and finally got my breakfast.

But as I turned around to find a place to sit, I bumped into another student and my plate slipped from my hands and crashed to the floor. The dining hall fell silent and it seemed everyone was looking at me. I turned a deep crimson. *Oh shit,* I thought. *Now everyone will think I'm a buffoon and stay away from me.* Then the entire assemblage began to applaud and hoot. A kitchen worker appeared and handed me another ticket while he cleaned up the mess. I got into the correct line and got #6 all over again.

Cautiously carrying my food, I saw a woman possibly waving at me. *Me?* I mimed. *Yes,* she mouthed, waving vigorously.

Setting my plate down on her table, I noticed that she looked to be about my age, early 30s, and had a constellation of freckles splashed across her cheeks and down her arms. Her short red hair was wiry, like a vegetable scrub brush that had been used on carrots.

"I bet you're new here," she laughed as she scooted her stool

7

closer to me. "That was quite a show-stopper you just gave."

"I'm still mortified." I didn't want to hear any more about it, and it annoyed me that she had pointed it out again. "Well, I think I heard you laughing the loudest."

"Probably. You should have gotten #5," she said tapping my plate with her spoon.

I wondered why she cared and I wished she wasn't sitting so close. "Why? Is it made with dragon eggs?"

"No, chicken," she said popping a sausage disk into her mouth.

"Well, I wanted #6." I slid my stool slightly away from her.

"You're American, right?" She put her hand on my shoulder.

"Yep," I said breaking my yolks over the rice. "This is an amazing place, there are so many different people." I shrugged a little, hoping she would remove her arm. "Say, what's with the loudspeakers at six in the morning, do you know?"

"They're political encouragements and physical training for the masses. They are bloody annoying, aren't they?" she said.

"I think they will be; this is the first time I've heard them."

"The same broadcast goes out to the entire country. When your Chinese gets better you'll be able to 'listen' between the lines of the announcements for political news."

"Are you a student here too? Where are you from?"

"I'm Australian. I graduated from this school two years ago. Now I teach English at Beijing University and live at the Friendship Hotel. I came to have a meeting with Ming, a teacher here." She finally moved her hand to the table.

"Hey, I just met her. She saved my life last night from a growly woman at the front door. This morning she gave me a tour of the campus."

"She's a good woman, a very good friend." She winked. "Good lookin' too, don't ya think?"

"Uh huh, please pass the soy sauce." Why was she asking me what I thought of Ming? Were they possibly together? Was

8

she obliquely asking me if I was into women, and was she? Her manner was unsettling, none too subtle, and I was beginning to wish I hadn't sat with her.

"Say, how come there are no Chinese people in here?" I was both curious and wanting to change the subject. "I look around and see a parade of colors, different ways of dress, and no Chinese people."

She tilted her head to the left and a half-knowing smile took over her lips. "There are several reasons, but the biggest is because it costs more to eat here. There's a Chinese side and there is a Muslim dining hall as well. You can go to the Chinese side, that won't be a problem. But you won't be welcomed in the Muslim hall unless you are a Muslim and then you would have to eat in the back and cover yourself up because you are a woman. Sounds like fun, huh?"

"I might try the Chinese side when I can speak a little."

"Don't wait for that, Yank. They will want to speak English with you since that's what they are studying. You won't be able to speak Chinese with them; they outnumber you. But they will be happy to trade slang with you, words your teachers will never teach you." She chuckled.

We both looked up when a two-by-two column of sixteen men marched into the dining hall. They all wore the same floppy gray jackets, boxy blue trousers and cheap blue sneakers. No one else seemed to notice them and she watched me watch them.

"What's that?"

"North Koreans. They always go around campus like that, marching everywhere. Don't talk to them. Their government calls Americans 'imperialist wolves,' and their 'Great Leader' is so unhappy with America. Every Saturday they go to their embassy for political study. If one of them is caught talking to an American, they must stand in front of the group and be humiliated."

"Holy smokes, then I certainly won't."

"I'm Elizabeth, by the way."

"Louise."

"I'll help you learn the ropes, if you want. Here is my card, give a call anytime. Let's have lunch in a few weeks, by then you will have a million questions. Oh, before you go and buy things for your room, check with the students who are leaving. It is an ex-pat tradition to pass stuff on to the new arrivals."

"Thanks. I'll call you sometime. Lunch sounds great." I was pretty sure I wouldn't call her.

"C'mon," she said taking my hand, "I'll show you how to bus the dishes."

I found my way back to Building #8. I was glad to be done with Elizabeth; she got into my personal space, too close for comfort. As I went through the double doors, I noticed a small area with a sliding window on my right, like a fast-food drive-up window. I saw the woman I had met last night, and went around to the door and knocked carefully.

She opened the door with a softer attitude.

"Are you Zhang?" I butchered her name, pronouncing it with a sound like *bang*.

"*Zhang,*" she corrected.

I tried to copy her sound, *Jaw-ung* and she laughed at my effort; she knew I was trying. She took my hand and walked us to the room I had slept in.

She began speaking in Chinese. I looked at her helplessly, spreading my palms up. She shook her head and laughed, then motioned for me to wait.

Just as she turned to leave, Ming arrived.

"We have decided that we will give you one of the best rooms in this building. It is on the third floor and you will have an American roommate. Zhang and I will help you move there now."

They each took a suitcase and I gathered up the blankets, sheets and the mystery pillow. The struggle up the stairs was

10

translated from English to Chinese and back again with all three of us laughing when Ming translated that Zhang said one of my suitcases could sink a water buffalo into the mud.

Ming opened the door to my room and I didn't see what was so special. It looked just like the one downstairs. Reading my face, she explained that this room got the best heat from the sun in the winter and the least heat in the summer. Additionally, she told me with a muted pride that my roommate's father was with the American embassy and that she would arrive in six weeks.

"Do you know when I can get my books? I really want to start my studies."

"Teacher Su will tell you this afternoon," she laughed softly. "I think soon."

What remained unsaid was that she had done something special for me, and I was surprised to find myself a little shy from her effort. She checked her watch and quickly handed me the door key. Then she took Zhang by the hand, and they left.

I stood alone in the spartan room that was now my home. I had left an apartment that had a fireplace, carpeting, soft furniture, a kitchen, and my own bathroom with a sit-down toilet. I was beginning to be tilted by the slam of sharp-edged changes. The food and getting it was new, no familiar faces, and no one to talk this day over with. I certainly did choose this world. But right then, for the first time, I questioned my decision. I wished I could talk to my friends at home, especially Eloise, about all of this, about today, a day that had rumbled with hundreds of tiny alterations. I missed her.

Since my roommate hadn't yet arrived, I chose the right side of the room and started putting my things away. After I finished making the bed, I got the pillow and carefully separated a little of the sewn end to see what the hell was in there. It could be little rocks or beans or maybe even cicada bodies. Finally I worked a small opening and found that it was filled with buckwheat, and not just the hulls, the whole damn grain.

It was nearly two o'clock and time to go meet teacher Su. Before I left, I took Elizabeth's card out of my pocket and tossed it into the empty desk drawer. My mind drifted to Ming's sweet smile. I wondered if Ming and Elizabeth were involved with each other. I was beginning to like Ming and hoped they weren't.

I stopped myself before the reverie could go too far. Julia was still a deep painful presence for me and I certainly wasn't going to get involved with anyone now, if ever. Back in the States Eloise had encouraged me to stay in Los Angeles, to meet someone new, and get over Julia. But I didn't want to meet anyone new; I just wanted to become proficient in Chinese and do it in Beijing.

I locked my door. Even though I was on the other side of the world now, it seemed I still couldn't get far enough away from Julia.

PEANUTS

花生米

For the first three weeks we spent our morning and afternoon classes in pronunciation drills. From eight o'clock until noon, then from two until four thirty we learned to curl our tongues, make guttural sounds, throw certain constructions up into our nasal cavities, and pronounce two "third tones" in a row. The grammar is without gender and verb-tense in which the past, present, and the future tense are inferred by context. This facilitates a blurring; this is not a side effect but a fundamental aspect of Mandarin.

I met students from many other countries; most were not English speakers, and I even had trouble understanding some of the Brits' English. The Palestinians, Somalis, Japanese, Egyptians, and Syrians and I could only communicate with nods and smiles. It would take more than six months before we could have simple conversations. Chinese became our common language.

At the end of the three weeks, we were given our textbooks. Finally, I thought, we could begin reading and writing. I was

13

arrogant. I assumed that since I had studied Mandarin at a community college and a church-sponsored weekly class for a year, I had a good grounding in beginning Chinese. I didn't. I had learned to write the complicated characters, and my grammar, verbs, and nouns were constructions from Singapore and Taiwan. But now I was learning the "official language." My dictionary was infused with the government's insular insistence on political expressions and overtones. That became apparent when I looked up the word *learn*. Yes, it was defined as acquiring a skill or knowledge, but the entry went on to explain that the best method of acquisition was through studying workers, soldiers, peasants, model communes, and the Communist Party.

A month in, we were given a rare afternoon off and I welcomed the early end of my school day. My mind drifted to Ming while I thumbed through the first several chapters of a textbook. I had seen her a few times around campus, but was too shy to go and talk with her. I had to be firm with myself and not allow that reverie. As I looked at the later chapters of Book One there was less of the Pinyin, the Romanization of the characters, and they became only characters. It unsettled me to read that the first lessons were based on the basic details of everyday life of a foreign student at the language institute. They knew too well when we got up, washed our clothes, took our meals, and studied.

There was a knock on my door, and as I began to stand to open it, Elizabeth barged in.

She looked around and shook her head. "Jeez, Louise, you need everything."

I was annoyed to see her, but she was right. I had no curtains, no covered lunch pot, and I had had to borrow a tin cup from my Italian neighbor to make coffee. "I haven't had time to shop," I said, defending myself. "We have been in class six days a week teaching our tongues and cheeks tantric activities."

"Hmmm, a tantric tongue. Nice thought," she said poking around in my bookcase. "Okay Louise, let's go. Do you have

14

shopping bags?"

"No, no bags. Why, where are we going?"

"Jeez-sus, honey, grab your wallet, your fat wallet. We are going shopping."

"I don't want to go shopping, I want to study."

"Nope, we're going shopping now because I'm here now. First, you're going to buy a hot plate."

"Why a hot plate? I don't want a hot plate; I want a fan. It's so damn hot."

"Because it gets bloody cold in the winter and the rooms have no heat. You can thank me later. The fans are sold out now. You have to buy when it's cold: that's why you're buying a hot plate today."

She stood in front of me, hands on her hips. A crooked smile spread. I knew I wasn't going to win this one.

"Oh for chrissakes then, let's go. But I still want a fan." I put my wallet into my pocket and asked, "Are you always so bossy?"

"So I've been told. You'll get used to it, then you'll love me."

She took my hand and we set off walking to the local village.

"I also need one nail and a hacksaw blade. I want to cut some bamboo for a clothes-drying rack and I want to punch holes in my thermos cup so I can make coffee."

"A hacksaw blade, one nail. Oh lordy." She turned slightly toward me. "Do you miss coffee?"

"Terribly," I said freeing my hand. "I brought a can from Los Angeles, but it won't last forever. Do you know where I can buy more?"

"At the Friendship Store, but it's awful. It tastes like ground-up pig knuckles and chicken toes."

"Gah. Yuck."

Laughing, she put her arm around my shoulder. "I'll ask a friend in Hong Kong to send a tin or two, if you'd like?"

I wasn't sure I wanted to be in her debt. The cost of reciprocity might be too high.

15

"No, no thank you. I'll ask a friend from home to send me some."

I slid out from under her arm and handed her a handkerchief. "Well, at least I have two of these," I said. "It's so damn humid."

"We're both sweating likes whores in a church," she said wiping her brow. "When are you going to get your bicycle?"

"Ming said she'd help me buy one next Saturday after class."

"She's good with her word. Have you talked with her much?"

"Not really, I just see her around. Ming did tell me I wouldn't be getting a roommate though, seems she decided to stay at Yale. Mostly we just smile and wave whenever we see each other."

"Hmmm," she hummed.

I checked her face. Were they together or not? I couldn't tell. I unnerved myself. Why did I need to know if they were a couple?

We must have been eye-openers for the people as we walked to the village: Elizabeth, tall and shapely, with her freckles and frizzy red hair, wearing a green blouse and khaki shorts; and me the same height, and a little rounder but with short, wavy blond hair, and wearing jeans and a blue blouse. A trailer carting maybe a dozen peasant women pulled by a converted rototiller belched blue smoke and noise. It slowed as it passed and twenty-four eyes were on us; some strained out of the trailer to keep looking at us as they motored on.

"Do the Chinese people stare at you all the time too?" I asked.

"Yeah, sometimes it gets bloody annoying. But usually I give 'em a big wink or slowly raise my skirt up my thigh. Try it."

"I can't imagine that you would wear skirts," I said.

"Only when it's really hot, they're cooler than pants."

The cicadas started up with their racket, so we continued walking in silence. After a few minutes their noise died down and I asked: "Why did you come here?"

"I was an English professor at the University of Adelaide.

After a few years, I transferred to the Singapore campus to teach and also study Mandarin."

"And then?"

"I fell in love with a visiting professor from Beijing. I followed her here and we had a scorching tumble for six months. That ended, and since I was already here, I came to the Institute, got my certificate two years ago, and now I teach English at Beijing University."

She was quiet for a moment, thoughtful; I saw a soft smile cross her face. I was surprised at how out she was with being a lesbian since she barely knew me, and it made me nervous. I didn't yet know the "special rules" of being out, dating, or courtship that gay people lived with, or probably under, in China.

We arrived at a large one-story building about the size of an American football field. There were scores of shoppers, and it seemed they all stopped to watch us.

"C'mon let's get some tableware, just bloody ignore them."

We leaned onto the display case, using it as a barrier against the gathering shoppers, and examined the cutlery. It was cheap, lightweight aluminum, easily a facile prop for a magician's act. I asked for two sets plus three serving spoons. Next I pointed to a brown enamel pot with a lid, two matching cups, and then some chopsticks. The shop assistant wrote down my items on a slip of paper, my soon-to-be receipt.

"What did she say?" I asked.

"She wants *yi quai ba*, a dollar eighty."

The assistant took my money, picked up my items and walked away; the murmur of the crowd intensified.

"She is wrapping up your stuff," Elizabeth said. "We can pick it up at the door, let's get your curtains next."

I looked where she pointed and again we had the attention of many other shoppers. I was uncomfortable and wanted them to mind their own business, but I noticed a kind old face on the edge of the crowd that didn't look away when my gaze met hers.

17

I nodded slightly, returning her smile.

"C'mon Louise, to the curtain fabric and—wait, stop here, buy a shopping bag."

"Elizabeth, the choice of stuff here is so cool. I just love the simplicity of it all."

"Louise, for chrissakes, it's junk, second-rate and third world."

"Au contraire, it's very utilitarian. What more could you ask for, Liz?"

She rolled her eyes and harrumphed. "Don't call me Liz. My name is Elizabeth."

"Got it," I chuckled.

I bought two cloth shopping bags and got them on the spot; this time there was no need to wait for the pickup near the door. The rules for purchase seemed capricious and unfathomable.

I let Elizabeth do all the talking at the fabric counter. She wanted me to get blue; I insisted on the deep green. I got the green. This too was somehow going to end up at the station near the door.

"C'mon, this way to the industrial section."

"Will the fans be there too?"

"Dammit, Louise, there are no more fans."

"Well, I'm going to look anyway."

The crowd was still following us around. Elizabeth told me they were chattering and delighted about the stuff we chose. Again I saw that the old woman was still meeting my gaze. I decided to speak to her.

"Wait a sec, I'm going to say hi to that old woman who keeps smiling at me."

As I walked over to her, the crowd leaned in to see what would happen next.

"*Lao nai nai*," I began, and the crowd of faces twisted away. Elizabeth was bending over, laughing loudly, and I stood there getting redder than the plastic chrysanthemums on the underwear and socks counter.

"What, what did I do?"

"You called her a sour glass of milk." Then she whacked me on my shoulder.

"Ah jeez, Elizabeth, do you have to enjoy my mistakes with such volume?"

"C'mon Louise, you're dangerous in public." Taking me by my wrist and still giggling, she aimed us to a smaller area in the back of the store.

This section looked like a large shed attached with bolts and steel plates to the main building. I could see daylight where the walls weren't tightly joined. The area smelled of welding gases, probably from a nearby acetylene torch. Here we found hot plates, D-cell batteries, saw blades, fan belts for rototillers, gaskets, screwdrivers, hammers, and nails. But no fans.

Hot plates came in four sizes, from useless to very big. All were pea green and had industrial construction, with no design aesthetics. "Get this one," Elizabeth said pointing at the next to the largest. "You don't want the biggest one, you'll blow the fuses in the dorm and everyone will hate you."

The assistant nodded and wrote the hot plate down on yet another slip of paper. "What else?" she asked.

"That and that," I replied in Chinese. The shop assistant looked at me. *Why on earth would this foreign woman want a hacksaw blade and one nail?* her face seemed to question. I had no words to explain it and Elizabeth didn't try.

"Oh god Louise, you are an adventure," she said taking the receipt from the woman. "Let's get your stuff and go back to the dorm."

We stopped at the front desk and paid the bill. Even though everything was expertly bundled with added string handles, we stuffed it all into the bags I had bought.

Each of us took a bag, and Elizabeth grilled me as we walked on.

"Okay," she said. "Your turn. Why did you come to Beijing?"

"I first came with some friends who were invited to teach a higher level of tennis to China's most talented players. This was a few months after Nixon and Mao opened our countries to each other." I wasn't sure if I wanted to discuss Julia, so I left that out. Shifting my bag to my other hand, I continued. "The first day in Beijing I fell in love with the sound of the language and the characters seemed magical. Simply put, I just wanted to learn Chinese, and maybe have a career as a simultaneous translator at the UN."

We stopped and put our bags down to wipe our faces and necks.

"So how did you make it happen?"

"It took a year to get accepted at the Institute and to get the visa. Toward the end of that year I sold everything and now, here I am."

"Why did you sell everything, why not storage? That's what I did. Put it all in a guesthouse on the ranch."

A guesthouse on her ranch? Her remark stung me; did she think she was better than me because she's wealthy? "Well, la di da. Did you pack it up in your Rolls and have your chauffeur drive it to the guesthouse?"

"Louise, what the hell?"

"All right, I get it, you have money, probably tons. I don't. I needed the money to pay for this, if you must know."

"So what do you want, a medal 'cause you're poor?"

My muscles tightened; I struggled to keep my voice from a scream.

"No, dammit. But money doesn't make you better than I am."

We stood silent, tense, gritting our teeth. We turned around when we heard our names called out.

"Louise, Elizabeth. I am coming."

Ming rode up to us, waving.

20

"You have been shopping," she said dismounting her bike. "Put your bags on my bike and we'll go together."

If she felt our tension, she didn't let on. We struggled to load the bags onto the back of her bike and finally ended up putting them over the handlebars. Before we started walking home we mopped our faces again. Elizabeth and Ming walked on the left side of her bike. I was on the other side, helping to steady the bike. They began to talk and laugh in Chinese. I couldn't understand them. Even though Ming occasionally glanced my way, I felt left out. Ming apparently preferred Elizabeth, a rich girl. How could I compete with that?

As we neared the guardhouse, the cicadas started up again and we lifted her bike over the three-inch pipe barrier without a word. Once the bugs quieted again, we sat together on a bench under a willow tree and complained about the heat.

"Come to my room," Ming suggested. "I have peanuts from my mother."

"Let's go," Elizabeth said jumping up. "Those peanuts are fabulous."

As we walked through the double doors, I said I would come to her room after I dropped off my purchases. Ming told me her room was just under mine, but on the first floor.

I took some time to examine my new things. I spent more time deciding if I wanted to join them. I felt like a third wheel. Even though I was curious about the fantastic peanuts, I decided not to go and began reading my textbooks and writing the simplified characters.

Maybe twenty minutes later there was a hard knock on my door. Figuring it was Elizabeth, I just spun around in my chair and waited for her to burst in. She did.

"What are you doing? We're waiting for you."

"I was looking at my new textbooks."

She rolled her eyes and puffed out a big breath. "Christ almighty, woman, you can do this another time."

She looked frustrated and shook her head as she walked over to my desk and put her hands over the edges. Leaning in toward me, but not as close as before, she took a breath. "Louise, you big dope, Ming invited you. She wants you there. Don't you see that? Just because you're miffed at me doesn't mean you can insult her. Now, c'mon goddammit, let's go."

I didn't want to say how I felt like an unmatched sock around them; it just seemed too complicated. And why was it so almighty important to Elizabeth that I go?

I looked down at my hands for a few seconds, and realized that I really did want to join them. "Well, since Ming wants me there, then I'll come."

Ming had pulled her desk to the center of the room and covered the top with newspaper onto which she poured a pile of roasted peanuts.

"Please sit, I'll be right back," Ming said.

I sat down across from Elizabeth who had gotten busy cracking and crunching peanuts. The tension between us seemed to be at a rolling simmer.

Ming pushed her door open and struggled in with a wooden chair. She pulled it up to the desk, where we all sat silent for a few awkward moments, intently shelling peanuts.

"Where are you going to buy the bike?" Elizabeth asked breaking the tension.

"We will go to Zhung Guan Cun, they have the best to choose," Ming said.

"How will you get there with just one bike?"

Looking at me, Ming suggested that we could walk there then ride home together.

I nodded.

"How's this for a plan?" Elizabeth put forward. "Let's meet at the dumpling restaurant in the village."

"I like this," Ming said scraping the shells into a pile.

Elizabeth looked up and asked, "Louise, you wanna

meet for lunch?"

Before I answered, I quickly considered if I wanted to spend more time with Elizabeth.

"I don't know, probably not."

"Oh cripes, Louise." She threw her head back and growled. "You are coming to lunch with us, and that's that."

Elizabeth went to use the building telephone to call a taxi, and Ming rolled up the newspaper and tossed it in a bin.

"You and Elizabeth seem very close," I ventured.

Ming laughed. "We are good friends."

What did that mean, "good friends"? How good?

"I'm not sure I want to have lunch. Maybe we could just get the bike and come back."

"Oh please," she said putting her hand on my arm, squeezing a little. "I really want you to come for lunch."

Her touch sent shivers and confusion. I wanted to leave.

"Maybe we could talk about this during the week then," I suggested moving toward the door.

"You can come and talk with me any time, feel free," she said opening her door. "You come to me here on Saturday after class."

"Okay," I said.

I bolted up the stairs and ran into my room. I needed to find faults in Ming. If I could find enough, then maybe I wouldn't like her, and if there weren't enough, then I'd invent them. I sat down at my desk, mind racing. *Let's see*, I thought. *She smacks her lips when she eats. She talks with her mouth full. She's probably a lousy kisser.*

HANDS

手

I put my new nail to good use punching holes in my aluminum thermos cup, which I lined with two squares of toilet paper. Now I could make coffee. Chinese toilet paper would be the perfect filter: textured like crepe paper, with no pigments.

Just before the water boiled, I put two scoops into my contraption, and thought about Ming. She did invite me to stop by anytime. But maybe she was just being polite, polite in a Chinese way that I was just getting to know. When an American student had asked Teacher Su if she could skip classes for a week to go to Shanghai, Su didn't say no, he said, "as you wish." Which really meant no. I slowly poured the hot water into the grounds and let them bloom.

Finishing off the coffee making, I told myself I was being ridiculous, it would be okay to just go and talk with her.

I sat with my cup, reading a Chinese children's book I had brought from the States. The sentences were simple, the grammar straightforward, good for a beginner. Then I remembered a singsong that I had heard some children of the Institute workers chanting. I'd copied it down on a slip of paper, and Ming would

24

know what it meant. I opened my wardrobe and fished out the paper from my blouse pocket and started for her room. Then I turned and sat down, opened my book, then closed it. I fiddled with a pencil. Opened and refolded the slip of paper. *C'mon Louise*, I told myself. *Just go.*

"*Jin lai*," was the answer to my soft knock. "Come in."

I pushed her door open just as she was pulling it and stumbled in toward her.

"Oh, Louise," she said as her left hand flew to her mouth. "Please come in."

She looked happy to see me. I blushed, I am sure, since this is something that comes all too easily to me.

"Am I bothering you? I can come another time if I am interrupting."

"No, I was just sewing. Not bothering."

She hustled another chair to her desk and slid her thread and needles into the desk drawer. Then she tossed the blouse she was mending on her pillow and pulled the big bag of peanuts from under the bed.

"Oh no, please," I said. "I don't want to impose on you. I just have a question."

"This is good that you came to see me. I like to talk with you."

I helped her spread out several layers of newspaper on the desk and she started to pour out the peanuts, but the bag got away from her and they went rushing out all over the desk and onto the cement floor. We both scrambled to stop the flow and catch the peanuts.

"Oh my," she said. "I hope you do not think I have bad manners."

"No, not at all," I said scooping up the peanuts into the bag.

She just stood there for a moment, embarrassed, looking down at the runaway peanuts.

Then she looked up and we both began to laugh, a laughter

that lightened the awkwardness, relieved the tension. We finished the task together, giggling.

We sat down across from each other, eating our runaway treats. I studied her fine, thin fingers, and I wanted to reach out and take her hand.

"What were you sewing?" I asked searching for something to say.

"Just my blouse bottom. I will lend you my needles if you need them."

"Thanks. Um, I heard some children singing something the other day and maybe you can tell me what they were saying," I said pulling the paper out of my pocket. "It was something like this:

"Wo ching le ni. Wo pang le pi. Wo chou si ni."

"No," she laughed. "It is this:

"Wo xing le ni. Wo fang li pi. Wo chou si ni. I salute you. I fart at you. I stink you to death. Be careful what you learn from the children," she laughed.

"Yes, I think I should," I said, again laughing easily with her.

"How about this expression? *Gai le mar le.*"

"Oh, you have a good ear," she said. "It is Beijing talk for 'you bet your boots.'"

"Would you mind teaching me Beijing words? They sound so different from Mandarin."

She handed me a peanut and said, *"gai le mar le."*

Sliding a peanut out of its red sheath, I wondered if we could also shop for other things when we went for the bike.

"I need a teapot to boil water and a frying pan. Would you mind if we looked for those too?"

"They will have these where we go, we can buy these."

"Good, thanks." Picking up a stray peanut from the floor, I realized I'd quickly exhausted my prepared topics of conversation. "Well," I said looking up, "I guess I should go."

"No need to go Louise, I like to talk with you. Please stay."

"I don't want to take your time."

"Well, if you must, then okay."

"I'll see you Saturday after class."

I needed to leave. Forces stronger than tides and gravity were pulling me to her. The newness of her and the familiarity of these lusty energies frightened me. Were she and Elizabeth together? Was she as kindhearted and trustworthy as I sensed? She seemed to like me, but what kind of like? I knew these feelings of attraction and I had no time for these diversions; learning Chinese and learning it very well would require monastic attention to my studies.

On Saturday, the pronunciation drills seemed to go on forever. The words that started with a *C* were difficult. We learned to start the sound by putting our tongues on the back of our closed teeth and then moving our tongues back quickly as our breath lightly exploded. Although I would barely admit it to myself, I was looking forward to spending time with Ming. I nearly ran to my room after class. I dumped my books and papers out of my army green satchel then tossed in my wallet, a small canteen of water, shopping bags, and my permission slip. Without that precious piece of paper I would not be allowed to buy a bicycle. Ming had such a sweet smile for me when she answered her door. She stuffed her shopping bag into her pocket and we took off for our two-mile trek to the larger village.

"Jeez, it's hot." We were sweating quite a lot by the time we reached the bike rack and Ming's bike. "How long does this heat last?"

"Less than one more month, then there will be more cool days than hot days."

"Do you have your permission slip?" she asked as we approached the gate and I bumped her bike over the three-inch barrier pipe.

"I do. You know, it seems like I need authorizations for everything."

As I took my turn pedaling with her on the back, she commented, "We all need permissions." She wrapped her arm around my waist. "But for you more times."

Her touch took my breath for a few seconds and when I took my turn riding on the back of the bike, I held her lightly, with restraint.

The heat was staggering. We realized that riding each other made us too hot so we decided to just walk to the village. Whole families on one bicycle buzzed past us, and donkey carts hauling watermelons struggled by. The smell of roasted garlic was in the air. Whenever I looked at her she seemed to get prettier. Her skin held a color that was like a soft gold. Once in a while our eyes met but we both quickly, shyly looked away.

The Zhung Guan Cun village seemed three times larger than Wu Dao Kou, the village near the Institute, and that many times more crowded and boisterous. Perhaps because this village was close to Beijing University, which had a good number of international students, people didn't stare. For once I wasn't a sideshow attraction.

Since it was Saturday, families were out shopping together; some had purpose, others browsed. Women walked with linked arms. Men were draped over each other, many holding hands. The main shopping building was as large as two airplane hangars, and ringed by peasants selling vegetables, fruits, roasted and raw peanuts, locally produced cloisonné, and small watercolor paintings.

Inside, the milling crowd and several large electric fans that hung from the ceiling stirred the heat. We found the two-cup aluminum teapot right away but it took a little longer to choose an aluminum frying pan. The shop assistant picked up my money, took the items, and walked away. Once again, the odd shopping rules.

"Stop here, you need this," Ming said pausing at a counter displaying candles and boxes of mysteries.

Although I knew I shouldn't have, I edged a little closer to her as we leaned on the counter.

"This will stop the mosquitoes," she said pointing to some thin square boxes. "Then use this if they bite you," she added, gesturing to stacks of small, round red tins.

Then she moved a little closer to me. I took in her sweet scent. My knees began to buckle a little.

We maintained that soft nearness as the shop assistant pulled out two flat boxes of what turned out to be coils of mosquito repellent. Ming moved even closer. What was she doing? If she was with Elizabeth, then this wasn't right. But, by god, I liked it. The assistant also handed her three short red pillar candles and a tin of Tiger Balm. This time she paid at the counter and stuffed them into her shopping bag. I gave her the money for my purchases and insisted on carrying them.

Pushing our way through the swarm of shoppers, we found the bicycle section. With her help, I found a Flying Pigeon that suited my height. I showed the clerk my permission slip and went to pay. When I returned, Ming was in an excited conversation with the shop assistant. She pointed at the bike, straightened up, and folded her arms over her chest. I wasn't sure if I should join them just yet, so I just waited several yards away.

The assistant left then returned with some tools and tightened the nuts on the brake levers, checked the chain, the tires and the pressures. When Ming relaxed her posture, I returned to them and handed the man my receipt. On the way out, we picked up my pot and pan, and then walked my new bike to the parking lot and secured it by hers, near the tallest camphor tree in the lot.

"Maybe we should go back in the store. Isn't there something else you want to buy or look at?" I asked. I didn't want to go to the restaurant. And I wasn't looking forward to seeing Elizabeth. Maybe we could find several more counters to lean against and slide together, stay close, just a little longer.

"No, no more shopping. I want to eat now."

Ming led the way to the restaurant and I lagged a few disappointed steps behind her. She pushed open two half doors that reminded me of an old saloon, except they were painted dusty green and one door hung slightly off its hinges. It was semi-dark, but Ming saw Elizabeth and someone else right away.

Ming introduced me to Guan, a physics teacher at Beijing University. The three of us walked across a sticky floor to the table where Elizabeth was waiting. I hoped folks didn't spit in restaurants too since they seemed to spit everywhere else. We sat down on simple wooden stools at a square table. A bamboo jar in the center held chopsticks and was sided by bottles of vinegar and soy sauce. No napkins. I took a peek at the floor, to look for snot balls. There weren't any, but as I pulled a stool from an adjoining table for my purchases I noticed spittoons placed in the corners of the room.

Elizabeth moved her stool closer to Guan, who had a thin face and braids about two inches longer than Ming's. Her smile held a subtle power, and a pair of black glasses framed her slightly wide-set eyes. She was dressed in a boxy navy blue suit and white blouse—frumpy, just like everybody else. She looked at me full on, quickly sizing me up, then giving me a slightly crooked smile. She scooted her stool closer to Elizabeth. She and Ming shared a quick eye-lock and Ming looked down shyly when she saw that I had noticed.

What was that about? I wondered. Were they taking my measure, or was it another communication entirely?

"Where are the menus?" I asked. I felt like I was floating outside of a circle, tethered but drifting. How were all of these people connected? I felt confused.

"There are no menus," Elizabeth answered. "You don't order what. You order how much."

Ming put her hand on my arm, and explained, "They only have the *jiao zi*, dumplings."

Guan and Ming had a quick conversation, and then stood

up. I watched them walk away.

"They are going to place the order at that window," Elizabeth said. "They'll bring the food and beer from that other window over there."

"How do they know how much we want?" I asked, still watching Ming, enjoying the way she moved.

"They don't, but they'll get six *liang*, about six ounces, for each of us. Do you like Chinese beer?"

"I don't know."

"It's bloody good."

"Guan is pretty and seems very nice," I said.

"She's a real good-looker, that's for sure. She's special actually."

I was quiet for a moment, not sure if I should express a new and accumulating intuition. I fidgeted with the chopsticks.

"Are you and Guan lovers?" I blurted. I immediately wished I could take that question back.

Elizabeth leaned forward, looked me straight in the eye, and answered, "Yes, we are."

I looked down at my hands, feeling my face bloom ever redder, not sure what to say. My thoughts started swimming. *This changes everything.*

I looked at Elizabeth; she had a goofy, knowing smile.

"I don't know what to say, I mean, all this time I thought that you and Ming were together."

"Christ on a stick, Louise," she said slapping the table with her hand. "You are one dense Yank. Do you have any idea how much work you've been?"

"What do you mean? What kind of work?"

"Oh my dear, dear Louise. I have been trying to get the two of you together for weeks. Remember when Ming invited us for peanuts and you were being a pill? I wanted to throw you down the stairs to her room."

"Was Ming in on all this?"

31

"Well, yes and…we'll talk later, they're coming back."

Ming arrived with four empty bowls and Guan carried two large bottles of beer and four glasses to our table. They went back to the window and Ming returned with a huge bowl of *jiao zi* and Guan carried a plate of boiled peanuts. I wanted to be alone, to breathe, to think. My heart was pounding from excitement and racing—from her and to her.

We passed the bowls and sauces between us, and each picked out a pair of chopsticks from the bamboo cylinder. Guan took the pair I had pulled out and wiped them on a clean cloth she pulled from her pocket, and then handed them back to me, showing me how to navigate yet another piece of my new life. Then she filled our glasses with beer from the bottles, which looked at least three times bigger than the ones back home.

Ming served the *jiao zi*, putting four in each bowl. After that, we each served each other. I hesitated to start eating. Although I had often used chopsticks before I came to Beijing, I wasn't sure I could manage the *jiao zi* with any skill. I watched how Ming used hers; they seemed like second hands for her. Well, I told myself, just go for it.

I slid the *jiao zi* around in a just-right mixture of vinegar and soy sauce and managed to eat them without mishap. We talked and laughed. I even found myself enjoying the way Ming smacked her lips; she seemed so happy. I learned from watching Guan how to serve the others before I took what I wanted. I passed the plate of peanuts around and I turned my chopsticks handle-side up and slid several nuts onto their plates, then my own.

I wanted to show off a little for Ming, so I picked up a single peanut with my chopsticks, but the nut flew away and landed in her beer glass. Everyone burst out laughing. I blushed yet again. Ming just fished it out with her chopsticks, popped it into her mouth with a flourish, and thanked me. We all laughed again, even me.

The four of us made our way to the bicycle parking lot, through the masses of shoppers that had grown even larger; their ruckus combined with the buzz of the cicadas was dizzying. There must have been two thousand bicycles. How anyone could ever find their own bike was mystifying. I silently thanked Ming for choosing that tall tree.

Ming and Guan walked arm in arm, ahead of Elizabeth and me, talking quietly in *Er Tu Hua*, the Beijing dialect. Nearing the parking lot, they said they were going off to buy something and Elizabeth tugged my arm and sat down on a bench. I sat down next to her.

"Would you like to come to my place for lunch in a couple of weeks?"

I drew circles in the dirt with my shoe, gathering my thoughts. "You know, two or three weeks ago I didn't want anything to do with you. I think I was jealous of you when I thought you were with Ming. But now I've met Guan and you seem so happy. I guess everything feels different and I see you in a new light. So yeah, absolutely, I'd love to come for lunch."

She put her arm around me and gave me a hug.

"Where are they going?" I asked, keeping a keen eye on Ming.

"Who knows? Probably to compare notes about you?"

"About me?"

"Cripes blondie," she whispered, "Ming really likes you, ya know."

I suddenly felt like a yacht with a careless skipper, a rudder forgotten. I sailed meridians in a few short moments.

"Louise, the look on your face. You didn't know?"

"I think I knew, but I wasn't sure enough." I slid my face between my hands. "Besides, these last several weeks I thought you two were together and that pretty much sealed the deal."

"Nice surprise, huh?"

"I've been here less than two months. China is overwhelming, living here is a challenge, studying is demanding. New friends, you, and now—and now her."

"Louise," she said patting my shoulder. "You're having the time of your life. Tell her you like her, tell her on the way home."

"Oh no, I just couldn't," I said slightly slumping over my knees.

"Alright then, I'll tell her for ya," she said bumping her knee into mine.

"Don't you dare," I said bumping her knee right back a little harder.

"Okay, okay I won't. Try using *xiao* in front of her name, mate. Call her *xiao* Ming."

"What kind of trouble are you fixing to get me into?" I asked.

"No trouble, honest," she said. "It's a term of endearment. The word has many meanings and levels of uses. In this case, it lets you say you really like her without being bold."

"That's soft, kind of gentle. I like it."

"Yep. And if it should come up, the Chinese word for gay is *tong xin*. Roughly, it means hearts in agreement. Nice word, eh?"

"Yeah, it is. Say, would you mind if I came over to your place next Friday night just to talk some more?"

"I'm going to Hong Kong on Wednesday and I'll be back Saturday morning. How about that afternoon?"

"That'll be good. I want to talk with you, I need to figure China out and her, I mean, Ming."

She patted my knee. "Just show up at four o'clock. I'll wait for you in the bar."

When Ming and Guan returned, they weren't carrying any purchases. Elizabeth caught my eye and raised an eyebrow. We each claimed our bikes, paid the one *fen*, less than a penny, parking fee, and said our goodbyes.

The late afternoon was cooler. The cicadas were silent. Whirring bicycle wheels, clopping donkey hooves, grunting men, and the quiet conversations of hundreds surrounded us.

Ming and I rode side by side at full-belly speed. I thanked her for helping me buy such a terrific bike. It felt sturdy and solid on the road. I liked my posture on this Flying Pigeon, my face up, and my back strong and proud.

When I looked at her she was smiling. She glowed with a wild light that I could not name.

Looking at me from the corner of her eye, she said, "I think you are happy."

We split apart to pass a man who had stopped his bike in the middle of the road to reposition his live chickens. Once again by her side, I said, "Yes, I am happy, very happy."

I didn't speak the whole truth. In fact, I was equally happy, scared, and uncharted. I had such a crush on her, but I didn't know how to navigate this society's manners. Did I ask her out? Where would we go? Were there places where lesbians went and felt safe and free? Did she have this lusty like for me as well?

"I am happy too," she said tilting her head a bit to the side, catching my eye, and then quickly looking away. Her smile, her color, framed in that drape of camphor and elm trees, was dazzling. The light was sensuous. I so wanted to touch her.

We rode past the public restrooms, held our noses and laughed. We remarked about the log yards of stacked raw lumber and the scores of coal chunk hills. Just after we thumped over the railroad tracks, I spotted a white ice cream cart and pointed.

"Let's stop here," I said.

I bought two popsicles, handed her one, and we walked our bikes into the shade of a deep green camphor tree, sitting down nearly facing each other on the butt-smoothed exposed roots. We couldn't pull the paper down quickly enough and the popsicles melted down our fingers. We leaned just a little more forward to avoid them dripping on our shoes.

"Ming?"

"Hmmm?"

I paused a moment and gathered my courage. "*Xiao* Ming?"

I could see her smile broaden; she lowered her head a little as she closed her eyes. When she opened them she looked at me. For the first time we gazed at each other without looking away. I felt my heart fall through my body and go deep into the earth where the roots of that tree found its essential substance.

After finishing our ice creams, and with two sticky fingers, I carefully pulled the small canteen of water out of my satchel.

"Xiao Ming, may I wash your hands?"

Without a word, she placed her hands, palms up, in my left hand. I poured some water, wedged the canteen between two roots, and gently cleaned her fingers.

She laughed softly and said, "Now I will wash you."

While she cleaned my hands, caressing them actually, much as I had done, I said, "Ming, I am *tong xin* too."

"Yes," she said. "I know."

DINNER

晚饭

Everything she stirred in my heart was equally terrifying and attractive. I decided to make a quick stop by her room on my way to dinner with Elizabeth. That would be a graceful excuse for seeing her.

"*Jin lai*," come in, she said, and I opened her door. She was towel-drying her hair. I had never seen her hair unbraided and she looked prettier, softer. I stood there taking her in. She cocked her head, smiling back at me.

"I wanted to thank you for suggesting this gift I have for Elizabeth, and I apologize for interrupting your beauty treatment," I said putting the box down on her desk.

"Not beauty, just cleaning. I am happy to see you."

I wanted to touch her but I was too anxious. I walked over to her kitchen area, which was really just the second bookcase on top of the second desk next to the wall. I looked at the tea tins, spices, cooking oil, sugar, and dried shrimps and eggs. Gluing myself to the floor, I also examined her pots and knives. I was trying to keep my heart rate from setting my hair on fire when she came and stood next to me.

"Lu."

I turned to her and instantly we slid into each other's arms. We hugged each other tighter, closer, exhaling a long breath at the same time. When she raised her face for a kiss, I took her face in my hands and pulled her to me. Our kiss was tender and powerful and I became undone.

I broke away. Stammering a "sorry." Stuttering half words, I aimed for the door.

"Was this wrong to kiss with you?" she asked, looking confused.

"No, it wasn't wrong, it was very right. I am, I am... just afraid."

"Maybe," she asked as we took the few steps to the door, "you will come to me after your dinner?"

Standing in the doorway, I said, "Maybe. Oh god, Ming, I don't know. I beg you to have patience with me."

When I turned into the hallway I realized I'd forgotten the box for Elizabeth. I stumbled back into the room, picked up the gift, and saw her smiling as she closed the door.

I bumped my bike over the three-inch diameter pipe placed at the gate to make sure all bicycle riders stopped at the guard station. The steel speed bumps were at every guard station, everywhere. I paused, pretending to check that my freight was still secured on the rack on my bike; I was trying to get my feet back under me. *Why did I leave so quickly?* How long, I wondered, would I let Julia's memory ruin things? Still feeling Ming's lips on mine, I swung my wobbly leg over the bike seat and set off to the west.

Trying to sync my speed with hundreds of other riders was folly; I rolled along slowly, catching my breath, catching my heart.

I slowed when I saw a large group of people congregating around the post office. I knew from experience that there might be something there worth watching. A few weeks earlier, a classmate from New Zealand and I had been riding our bikes north of our institute when we saw a similar crowd. At the center of that one, two young boys were drumming paradiddles on upturned plastic buckets. Then an older man and a younger fellow pulled snakes out of their mouths. The reptiles had slithered into their noses, and then exited their mouths with snot and fanfare. I rolled up to this crowd anticipating another spectacle.

But it soon became apparent that this wasn't a countryside circus act. People were bartering stamps. Still, it was interesting that I would recall an event that matched my state of mind—rambunctious, wild, and intoxicating.

A young fellow approached me; his forwardness made me wary. He was smooth in his demeanor, with a swipe of hormonal pimples on his forehead, and a charming smile. He was tall and gangly, even by northern Chinese standards. His big feet accentuated his loping gait, yet his hands were elegant enough to play a piano.

"Do you want stamp?" he asked in struggling English.

Taking a half step back from him, I said in Chinese, "I don't know, I don't know anything about this." *What would Ming do?* I wondered.

"Get book with pictures."

"A book with pictures. Hmm, do you mean a catalogue?"

"Yes, buy that. You want this stamp now? Very pretty."

The crowd began to focus on us and I wasn't sure if bartering stamps was legal, so I hurried the transaction.

"I'll buy it. My name is Louise, what shall I call you?"

"Wang."

I had no idea what it was worth, and suspected that I was being conned, especially when the crowd began to laugh, and other sellers began tapping me on the shoulder, shoving stamps in front of me. I became overwhelmed and wanted to leave, but the crowd had grown larger, more demanding. I began to feel nervous and looked for a path to my bike. I wished Ming were with me, to explain things, and protect me so I wouldn't be alarmed.

Nearing panic, I just pushed my way through the people to the parking lot.

Just as I got on my bike, I saw Wang again. He gave me a sweet smile and waved. I decided I should ask Elizabeth or maybe Ming about this guy and the stamp collectors.

Quickly rejoining the other riders, I pedaled west, and then turned south. About a mile from the hotel Ming again bustled in my attention. She was hard-stirring my heart. Our kiss still wobbled me, and I wasn't sure if I was ready for what seemed possible with her.

Arriving at Elizabeth's hotel, I dismounted my bike and walked it over the pipe at the guard station, locked it, and carried my gift into the grand lobby, which was carpeted in pink and green pastels. The chandeliers and wall sconces softened the tone of the bold colored murals that were "revolutionary" in spirit. How lavish it seemed to walk on carpet instead of cement and be surrounded by colors other than dusty blue. I felt washed in old familiars and amused to realize how comfortable I was becoming with my new austere living conditions.

Nearing the bar, I smelled that ubiquitous mix of whiskey and cigarettes to be found in any well-attended urban lounge. I saw Elizabeth and we waved.

She cradled my elbow as we walked through a side door and onto a white latticework portico.

"I am making tacos for dinner, something American for you. How does that sound, mate?"

"Oh my god, it seems like forever since I have eaten anything like that."

"I just got back this morning." She smiled, taking my wrist. "I bought cheeses, spices, hamburger, and taco shells, all the things that are not to be had in this ancient city."

A left turn took us out of the portico, and into a short, brightly lit hallway. I felt slightly awkward to be with her and making a new friendship. I hoped I wouldn't drop or spill anything or act like a doofus.

"Here we are, my humble home. Make yourself comfortable."

Her living room had muted celadon-print rugs on the cement floor and the air was cool. The sofa and a pair of matching club chairs were upholstered in doe-colored leather. She snapped on two floor lamps and the room softened to a welcoming glow.

"Elizabeth, I brought you some scotch. A friend of yours told me you like Glenlivet, was she right?"

"Yes, she was. Let's crack it. Do you like it neat?"

"I prefer ice if you have it and just a little will do."

"Who is this well-informed friend of mine?" she chuckled as she went into the kitchen.

Easing myself down into the blessed remembered comfort of a sofa, I said a little louder, "Ming. I told her I was going to have dinner with you and I asked her what you liked to drink."

"Good on 'er, she's right."

Handing me a glass with several ice cubes and pouring until I said a quick "whoa," she set the bottle on the simple elm coffee table, and settled back on the sofa. We clinked glasses and toasted our new friendship.

"Something happened on my way here that worries me a little. Can I check it out with you?"

She nodded while she sipped her scotch.

I recounted meeting Wang and the other stamp traders. When I finished she set her glass down.

"In late '78 there was a movement called The Democracy Wall. The people put up posters in the Xi Dan district agitating for democracy, and soon after, it started to spread all over Beijing and then to other cities too. It only lasted a year before the commies shut the bloody thing down. Guan told me that the faithful still secretly meet at post offices under

41

the guise of trading stamps."

"So, maybe I shouldn't go there?"

"You can go buy stamps if you want. Just watch what you talk about and with whom."

Feeling a little calmer, I took a sip of scotch.

"Your furniture is wonderful and comfortable. Where did you buy it, the Friendship Store?"

"Nah, mate, I had it shipped here from Adelaide."

"Elizabeth, somehow I'm not surprised. I like your colors. You've made a nice cozy home."

"Thank you. How about more ice?" she asked rising from the sofa. "I'll just get a few more cubes. And I've got some nibbles too."

From the kitchen she sang out, "By the way, Ming asked me about you that day I met you. She wanted to know if I thought you also liked girls."

"What did you say?"

"I told her I didn't know for sure, but I thought so. She sure was curious about you. I decided then that I should get you two together."

"Well, you certainly did that. Did she have a hand in your shenanigans?"

She plopped two more ice cubes into my glass and set down a plate of crackers, a shallow bowl of Vegemite, and a plate of chicken feet.

"Not really. It was my idea but she liked that I was on a mission to find out about you."

"Do you know if Ming is seeing anyone?" Ignoring the chicken feet, I reached for a cracker and held my breath, hoping for good news.

"No, I don't think she is, been more than a year now since she dated a doctor." She poured a little more scotch for herself. "So, did you kiss her yet?"

I almost choked on the scotch sliding down my throat;

gulping peaty air, I managed only a mumble. Her boldness had caught me off guard, but it wasn't as bothersome as before. I wasn't sure I could totally trust her yet, but thought I might take a chance.

"Wadya say?" Turning to me she said, "Louise, you're blushing."

"No, no, it's the scotch."

"Bullshit, you did kiss her."

"All right, yes we did. We kissed for the first time before I came here," I said pouring a little more whiskey into my glass.

"So, how come you weren't late?"

Okay, I thought, *I'll just tell her as much as I'm comfortable saying.* "I had to leave. It's too much for me right now."

"What do you mean 'too much'?"

"There was a woman back home, Julia. We lived together for almost five years. One day I came home from work and she had left a note, saying she left me for my best friend." The memory caught in my throat and my lips began to tremble.

"Hold on, mate, you don't have to tell me if it's too hard to talk about."

"Just give me a second, I think I want you to know."

"Take your time."

"She was just gone, it was so sudden. We talked once briefly, when she came for a few forgotten items, but we never talked about what had happened. Maybe we could have worked things out, but probably not. I was angry and depressed for months. After that I swore I'd never love someone so deeply, so strongly again."

"So now Ming is coming into your life and you're scared shitless, right?"

"Yeah, I sure am."

"Ya wanna know what I think? Just get over it already. Julia was a long time ago, it's time to move on, for chrissakes."

I was taken aback by her curtness and my face must have

43

shown surprise.

"Oh shit, there I go again being an insensitive lout. I'm sorry, mate. Sometimes my words don't match my feelings. What I meant to say was go for it. Ming is worth the chance. After Guan, there is no finer woman. Just give her your heart. It'll be okay."

I considered her encouragement; maybe it would be okay to let my heart go. *Maybe.*

"Thanks, thanks for listening. I appreciate it."

"Of course. C'mon, mate, grab your glass and let's get cooking."

Her small kitchen had a refrigerator, propane stove, and a small island in the middle of the brown cement floor. There was even a three-foot square window framed with taupe-painted cupboards over the sink that looked out onto bike racks.

"Will ya look at this? You have a real kitchen, and a sink too. You don't have to schlep your dishes down the hall to wash them and hope that the sink isn't full of pig guts and that there is still hot water. My god, Elizabeth, some Burundi students slaughtered a pig in the laundry room last Saturday. There were pig parts and blood everywhere."

"Cripes, I remember those days. That's fuckin' inconsiderate, if you ask me." Opening a drawer and handing me a shredder, she said, "The cheese is in the fridge, and grab the onions for me, will you please?"

"How is it that you, Guan, Ming and I guess some others are so out here?" I asked, unwrapping the cheese.

"We are a small community. We are discreet and take care of each other," she answered, taking up an onion, rubbing off the skin. "As long as we don't organize a dykes-on-bikes parade down Heavenly Peace Boulevard, we are left alone. We're mostly invisible like women everywhere."

"I like how women and men are so openly affectionate with each other, makes it easy to hold hands with someone you like, I bet."

"Yep, but don't go smooching in public," she said. "Keep it subtle. Do you need more ice? Help yourself to the scotch. Like I was saying, China is opening up, life is becoming a little more free. But it's only a start, so be careful about being too out."

"I am good with the scotch," I said. "What could happen if we are caught as lesbians, or do something improper?"

"We'd probably get kicked out of China, maybe sent to prison and bust rocks all day. I only hear rumors, and I sure as hell don't want to find out."

I held my breath for a few nervous seconds. "How will I know what is okay to do in public or private? Do neighbors get nosy and tell the cadres about what they hear or see?"

"Neighbors are nosy everywhere. Just follow Ming's lead; she knows how things go. After awhile you'll get it."

I washed my hands, and then rinsed the lettuce and tomatoes. "I want to ask her out, but I don't know where we'd go. Is there a restaurant or a disco or somewhere safe I could take her for a date?"

"There isn't much, mate. Mostly walks and bike rides. Maybe a picnic when the weather's good." She took up a second onion, and paused. I looked at her and she teased, "You could always do laundry together, or jigsaw puzzles."

"Jigsaw puzzles, very funny. I want to give her the best, you know."

"I can see that all over your face," she giggled, as she chopped.

"You know something, a couple of days ago I went to see Ming in her office during the morning break and to ask about what to bring to you. We sat there just looking at each other."

"Hmmm," she said smiling.

"I couldn't leave and I almost couldn't bear to stay any longer. Finally she asked me if she could call me Lu. I said sure, why? She said because Louise had too many letters for her mouth."

"That sounds like her," Elizabeth chuckled, adding the

hamburger and spices to the onion she'd dumped in a skillet.

"Then we giggled together like schoolgirls, and thankfully that broke the spell and I had to run fast back to class."

"Oh lordy, Lu. You've got it bad. May I also call you Lu?"

"Yeah, that's fine."

"Where's that cleaver?" I asked. "I want to chop the tomatoes. God this kitchen smells like really good food."

"It's there by the sink."

I finished filling two bowls with lettuce and tomatoes. I stopped and turned toward her. "What do you think of taking her to gay night at the Forbidden City?"

"Now that's a bloody good idea. We'll double date." She rolled her eyes.

"Blondie, just grab those bowls will ya and let's eat. The table's in the front room, c'mon."

Balancing the cheese, lettuce and tomato bowls on themselves and feeling just a bit unsteady, I followed her to a classic square Chinese dining table, the style favored by peasants, elm wood with a lightly lacquered finish. Putting the bowls down, I told her how much I admired her table.

"Ain't she a beaut? I'll just light some candles and we'll eat."

Biting into those tacos was glorious. With each crunch, I could feel the distance between my old American life and my new Chinese life. The flavors, sounds, and textures were luxurious, almost foreign now, providing a contrast that mirrored the shift of my sensibilities. I was embracing my life here. I was happy, and maybe even, becoming happier.

We lingered over the meal, contentedly scraping up the last bits from every bowl.

"So Lu, pretty fuckin' good tacos, eh?"

"Yeah they're marvelous. How did you get the hamburger here from Hong Kong?"

"Well, I rang up an old girlfriend…"

"You are some Sailorina, Elizabeth. A girl in every port."

"Jealous, Lu?" She laughed. "I asked her to buy the best she could find, wrap the meat in plastic wrap, freeze it, and then put plain brown paper around the whole package. When we met for dim sum, she gave it to me and I put it in my suitcase. Then she took me to the airport. Good, eh?"

"You are amazing, Elizabeth."

Reaching into the cupboard for crystal snifters, she said: "Have a finger of cognac. It'll be our dessert, and it will keep you warm for your ride home. Take these glasses and go put your arse on the sofa."

"No, no more for me, thanks." All I really wanted was to hold Ming again for a proper kiss.

Elizabeth returned with a bottle of Camus Cuvee, sat down next to me on the sofa, and poured cognac into her glass. I smiled. I really was having fun.

"Elizabeth, this has been a wonderful evening, I can't thank you enough for the comfort, your kindness, your advice. And viva your tacos."

"You're very welcome, I'm really liking you too, Lu." Sipping her cognac, she asked, "What're ya gonna do about Ming?"

"I really don't know." I paused. "Well, that's not exactly true. I hear a strong voice that says to just let myself get to know her, let her know me back."

"Ya know, mate, sometimes things do work out without a heartbreak or a betrayal."

I thought about that for a few moments. "Maybe, maybe I just might want to find out."

We rose from the sofa together, and she gave me a full-on hug and a kiss on my cheek before helping me into my jacket. I hugged and kissed her back.

"Be safe going home. You are always welcome here and call me anytime you want," she said taking my hand. "See ya soon, mate."

"Thanks, I will. The same for you—you know our number."

We laughed since there was only one cheap plastic telephone in each building.

Hurrying into the now cool night, I found my bike, unlocked it and bounced it over the pipe. Swinging my right leg over the seat, I headed east. It was chilly; I could smell the cusp of autumn. I suddenly found myself pedaling hard, going as fast as I could. I laughed at myself. If Ming and I could sometimes take little, careful steps, maybe everything would be okay. I put on even more speed.

She was standing in the doorway of the TV room when I got home, and I wondered if she had been waiting for me. I walked up behind her; she smelled like jasmine. She reached back and took my chilled right hand into hers. I received her warmth, leaning just a little closer, and whispered in her ear.

"May I come to your room now and talk?"

"Yes, now."

I followed her down the hall, feeling the ebb of my courage, nearly sure that I would become unable to speak. She opened her door and motioned for me to sit at her desk.

"Would you like some water?"

I nodded. She poured hot water from her thermos into two white porcelain cups and set them down on the desk, taking a seat opposite me.

She reached for my hand. I looked at her hand in mine and held her fine, thin fingers.

"Lu, I think maybe someone hurt you very deep and that is why you are afraid."

My chin trembled and I tried to stifle a whimper.

"Come to me over there, so I can be closer."

We sat down on her bed and she put her arm around me. The story of Julia poured out, all of it, the mess of it, the anger, the pain, and the fears. And still she held me. When I was finished she handed me some toilet paper and I blew my nose.

We sat together while I calmed myself. Then we lay down

next to each other. My head was on her chest and I listened to her heartbeat. She traced the contours of my ear.

"Are you still afraid?"

"A little, but not as much. I might become afraid again, but I'll try not to. We might have to go slow sometimes. Is that okay with you?"

"This is okay. We can do this."

We lay together quietly for a while. I took in her caresses, returned them.

"Do you want to leave now?"

"Not really."

I felt my soul begin to rest, to relax. Not completely, just enough. I closed my eyes and took in her sweet scent, felt her braid tickle my cheek.

"Is there someplace we can go together, kind of like a date? Someplace where we can dance or be alone and safe?"

"Yes," she said popping up onto her elbow. "We can eat outside food together. I know where to go."

Outside food? I wondered. "Do you mean a picnic?"

"Yes, that is what I mean." She giggled. "How about next Saturday? We can plan during this week."

We fell quiet. Our eyes held each other's gaze for long moments, our breathing came in shorter puffs.

"I want to kiss with you," she whispered. "I like to do this with you very much. Will you stay with me for a little while?"

GARDEN OF PERFECT BRIGHTNESS

袁明元

I knew how to wash socks and underwear, but big things like sheets and jeans were beyond my skills, and I wrote my grandmother to ask for help. Her letter, with detailed instructions on how to hand-wash clothes, also ribbed me about my predicament. *Household abilities seem to have drifted away in these modern times,* she wrote. I knew one thing for sure: I would never wear jeans again as long as I lived in China. Washing them was like heaving a dead horse in and out of a trough.

I decided that I would take myself to Zhung Guan Cun, the far village, and buy some Chinese cotton pants. I would go alone, no Ming or Elizabeth to help me with the purchase.

I made the familiar ride and parked by the tree Ming and I had used as a landmark several weeks earlier. Since it was a Wednesday, shoppers numbered in the hundreds instead of thousands and it was easy to go straight to the pants section. The assistant in the women's section, seeing that I was taller than most women, instantly waved me away, pointing me to the men's section.

Looking up from a display case that offered pants in only

green or blue, I opened my hands in a helpless gesture at the approach of the female assistant. With a questioning face, I asked for two, in Chinese, and pointed at the blue pants. She eyeballed my size and handed me two pairs. I think she said I could return them if they didn't fit, since there were no try-on rooms. But she may have offered me free alterations for all I understood.

Riding home I felt a new confidence. I had done this on my own and I was thrilled. Pedaling with the masses gave me just the right speed to think about my studies. I was encouraged with my progress and, although it was unfamiliar to learn by memorization and mind-numbing repetitions, it seemed to be working. We were being assigned fifteen new words to be able to pronounce, read and write each day, and I was keeping up. Next week it would increase to twenty, and I was determined to continue doing well.

I decided to ride the long way around the campus before returning to my homework. I slowed as I passed the hedges and flowers around the display cases of students' calligraphy. The flowers still smelled sweet as they had when I walked there with Ming my first morning at school, but it was getting cooler and less humid. The cicadas were gone now, burrowed deep, awaiting their annual wake-up call. Making the final turn toward Building #8, I saw Ming up ahead. Her gait was distinctive, a bit out-toed, giving her a slight waddle. I slowed and enjoyed watching her talk with two Norwegian students. Her gestures were kind and she made the students laugh. Having now mastered the art of slowing, stopping, and smoothly dismounting my bike in one motion, I glided to her side after the students waved their goodbyes.

"Lu," she said, an inhaled breath and a smile arriving all at once. "I'm glad to see you. Where are you going?"

I had learned that Chinese people don't say, "Hi, how are you?" when they see you, they ask, "Where are you going?" or "Have you eaten?" The latter greeting seems to have grown from centuries of ordinary folks often not having enough to eat.

"I just bought some pants at Zhung Guan Cun."

Chuckling, she said, "I think they must be men's pants."

"How did you know?"

"You are taller than me and I have the last women's size. Easy."

She slipped her arm into mine as we laughed and walked together.

"Lu, I want to give you something," she said pulling me closer to her side. "May I come to your room when we get back?"

"Sure, you want some coffee?" I wondered if she knew the effect she was having on my heart rate.

"I don't know this, I will try."

"Okay, see you in a few."

I closed my door and went straight for my last can of Yuban. Eloise, my friend in Los Angeles, had promised a care package with two cans of coffee and they should arrive soon. Opening the top, I could see that I had enough for three, maybe four more cups. I pulled out the hot plate and plugged it in, and then decided to try on my new pants. One pair fit perfectly, the second pair had one leg shorter than the other. That meant I would have to go back to that far village and exchange them.

I started to get nervous, fidgety, thinking of Ming. I reminded myself I could be fragile and strong and scared and brave all at the same time. Pulling my desk chair near the hot plate, I filled the aluminum teapot, and put three scoops of my precious coffee into my converted thermos cap. I sat down on the chair and waited for the water to boil. With my elbows on my knees, my face in my cupped hands, I imagined, and not for the first time, what it would be like to make love with her.

The steam began to come out of the little spout when she knocked then banged open the door.

"Lu, I am here."

Standing up from my chair, I saw that she was holding two small wooden structures as she came through the door.

"This one is for you," she said of the little stool, handing it to me. "The other one is for me to sit next to you now, but I'll take it away when I go."

We set the stools down and embraced. She just fit so right. We began kissing. Touching tentatively.

I forgot about the teapot on the hot plate and when the top popped off with a *whoosh*, it startled both of us.

"*Xia si wo*, that scared me to death," she said throwing her arms across her chest.

I retrieved the lid and put it back on the pot while we both laughed. "Let's give your gift a test drive," I said putting the chair back at my desk and unplugging the hot plate.

I examined the stool's simple construction. Measured by my eye, it was about a foot high, with a seat that was 8" by 5". The pine surface had chips and gouges on the two wide legs, but the top surface was smooth, probably from hours of sitting.

"Where did these come from?" I asked pouring the water into my coffee maker.

"We used them when we went to political meetings. Sometimes the old cadre would talk for hours, so we had something to sit on. Everyone has them."

"Thank you. This will make my cooking life so much easier."

"Yes, I know this."

While I was pouring the coffee into the cups, I noticed that she had pulled my stool closer to her. When I handed her a cup, I moved it a little further away with my foot.

"How is it, good?" I asked sitting down on the stool that I had managed to get another inch further from her.

"Lu," she said scrunching her face, "I don't like this."

Oh no, how could she not like coffee? Julia and I loved coffee together, especially on Sunday mornings with the newspaper.

"Do you want some water to make it weaker, maybe some sugar?"

"No, I don't like it." She spat her mouthful back into the cup.

53

I wished she hadn't done that. My prized coffee. I had considered saving hers for later, but not anymore.

"Would you like some tea instead?" I hoped my annoyance wasn't obvious.

"I think I would like that better."

I stood up to plug in the hot plate again and poured more water into the teapot, then scooted the stool even further from her. She noticed my little bench maneuvers, but said nothing.

"Lu, how did you make that bamboo stay up?"

I looked where she was pointing and saw she was admiring my bamboo clothes drying rack, the one I had crafted with my hacksaw blade. She reached out and pulled my tiny backless chair right next to hers and harrumphed.

"That is very good," she said. "Will you make one for me?"

"Of course, I would be happy to."

Handing her a cup of jasmine tea, I sat down on the stool that was now right next to her again. We looked at each other and giggled at the dance of the stools.

"Have you been to the Garden of Perfect Brightness? It's near the Summer Palace," she asked, smiling at the taste of tea.

"No, just the tourist part of the Summer Palace, in 1980."

"We will go there for our picnic."

"I'm really looking forward to it," I said softly, surprising myself with the depth of my reply. "What can I bring? How about yogurt?"

"Yes, this is good. I will come to your room after your class to pick you up."

She spun a quarter way around on her stool and pulled me to her. She took my face into her hands and gave me a big, fat kiss. I took her into my arms and leaned her back like a flamenco dancer and kissed her all over her neck and face.

"Oh, Lu, you are so good at this," she said, fanning herself with her hand as she straightened herself back on her stool.

While she composed herself, she asked me to bring spoons

and chopsticks for two. Then she stood, picked up her stool, and moved to the door. She hesitated a moment and half turned back. She faced me and held my eyes with hers just a little more deeply than ever before. Then she left.

I plopped myself onto my bed and took deep breaths, resting my hands on my heart just so it wouldn't fly away. *Ming.* I loved saying her name. It meant "a bright, brilliant light." *See,* I told myself. *You're still in one piece. Everything will be okay.*

We left home mid-afternoon that Saturday and arrived at the Summer Palace some thirty minutes later. We parked our bikes and carried our shopping bags, hers with food, mine with a sheet, a canteen of water, chopsticks, spoons and yogurt. As we walked to a less crowded area to the north, a place that Beijingers called The Ruins, Ming told me that in 1860 the French and British had burned down that section of the Summer Palace. Three years later, the Dowager Empress restored the buildings except for this section, which is called, fittingly, The Ruins of the Summer Palace.

We turned east for another ten minutes, passing several small lily ponds. The foliage grew denser. We climbed up a small hill to its flattened top. Miraculously, we'd arrived at a place without another soul.

"Here we stop," she said.

I took out the sheet and together we placed it on the soft grass. From her bag, she pulled three small pots, their lids tied down with plastic string. She had prepared perfectly sliced, lightly salted cucumbers in one pot, sliced red bell peppers and turnips in oil and vinegar in another, and precisely cubed watermelon in the last. I laid out the yogurt in the center of the sheet, the spoons and chopsticks. And, of course, she had brought a small bag of peanuts.

We sat crossed-legged next to each other with our feast in front of us. We glanced at each other now and then, smiled and often leaned on each other as we took up a vegetable with our chopsticks.

"These vegetables are delicious. Will you teach me how to prepare them?"

She looked so pleased with my compliment, and said, "Of course, I would be happy to teach you everything I know."

I was quiet for a minute. There was something I had been curious about and decided to ask her.

"Ming, have you been in love before?"

A quick look of surprise passed over her face, and then she looked down. I thought I had asked an insensitive question and began to wish I could take it back.

"I'm sorry, I didn't mean to put you on the spot. You don't have to answer."

"I will answer you. Sometimes I don't talk right away because I need to find my English words to say." She handed me the bag of peanuts. "When I was in college, my roommate and I were together during that time. We thought we were in love. We called it that. But now I'm older and I think we were just deep friends and liked sex together. After that maybe I had two more girlfriends. More than a year ago I met a doctor in a nearby work unit. We were good together for a while but I noticed she was haughty."

"What do you mean?" I put the bag of peanuts down.

"She was rude to shop assistants. Maybe she thought she was better than they were. Her parents suffered during the Cultural Revolution, so I think that made her heart afraid to seem ordinary. I haven't seen her in a long time."

She looked as though there was more she wanted to say. Instead she squeezed my hand, said she'd be right back and went to find a place to pee. I walked a few yards away to pick a small bouquet of wild flowers. Returning to the sheet, I rolled onto my back. It was late afternoon and the sky was beginning to give up its blue, the clouds hinting gold and cinnabar.

Ming stood above me when she returned and was edged

in that play of light. For the first time, finally, I could name her color: she held the colors of early sunset, *Wan Xia*. I couldn't take my eyes from her.

Her voice rang playful, yet deeper than I understood.

"You think I am beautiful."

"I sure do."

She sat down close to me and I handed her the small bunch of wildflowers. She received them as if I had given her imperial jewels from the Empress herself. She took my hand, and looked at me full on, holding me with her eyes, and gently kissed my hand. I leaned over to her, took her face in one hand and kissed her fully, softly on her lips. We were stunned by the power of that tiny kiss. We caressed and kissed each other as the light edged to early evening.

"Let's go now to my room," she said jumping up, "let's ride as fast as the wind."

I wanted to go with her, to touch her, feel her body next to mine, but I couldn't move. Fear was twisting and spinning, right alongside my desire for her.

"Let's go now, Lu." Looking down, she asked, "Lu?"

I took her hand and pulled her back down to a sitting position next to me.

"What is the matter?" Her lower lip began to tremble. "Maybe you don't want me?"

"Oh, Ming. I want you so much. Maybe I can say I'm almost in love with you. I am so afraid to let my heart go to you, afraid that I would break into tiny pieces and then you would just disappear."

We remained quiet. A few of her tears dripped on my hand. She spoke.

"Lu, I want you deeper in my heart. I want to touch all of your body, and you to touch me. But again you are afraid." She started banging her pots together as she gathered them up, and then stopped. Looking at me with reddening eyes, she said,

"When you are not so much afraid, then you come to me."

We packed up the picnic and walked back to the bicycle parking lot, paid the fee and started home. I rode just behind her through the crowds of other bicycle riders. We didn't talk. I didn't have anything to say, not until I could find the courage to let go of the memory of Julia. I wondered if I could.

I walked Ming to her door and she said, "You stop here. You can come to me when your heart is free."

"But, Ming, I want…"

"No, I don't want you now. You go," she said closing her door on me. I stood a moment alone in the hallway.

I dragged myself away from her closed door and went up to my room. I turned on the desk lamp, poured a glass of water and plugged in my hot plate. I pulled the short wooden stool from under the desk closer to the glowing coils and sat down. *I may have lost her forever now,* I thought, and cursed myself for my fear. I flopped down on my bed and started to cry, washed with waves of sadness and then anger. "Well, to hell with them both," I said out loud. *I came here to study, not fall in love. So maybe it's for the better that Ming is gone.* I got up, washed my face and went to the dining hall.

For several days I avoided seeing her. I left early for school, didn't go to her office at class breaks, and I lingered in the dining hall after meals. The tensile strength of my ambivalence was formidable. I found I could concentrate on my homework only if I did what my fellow Chinese students did: walk around campus in the evening and read my lessons out loud. If I couldn't solve the problem of my heart, at least I wouldn't fall behind in my studies.

By Wednesday afternoon my resolve began to waiver. I missed her, the smell and feel of her. But I stopped myself. Thursday the tug was stronger, and still I held back. During breakfast on Friday morning, I decided to ask her to walk with me after dinner.

But as I returned to my room after class, I noticed her bicycle was missing. Several times on Friday and Saturday I knocked on her door, but she still wasn't home.

Before I fell asleep Saturday night I worried. Maybe, when she told me she didn't want me, she meant forever.

On Sunday I checked her room several times more. I was feeling disheartened and even frantic when there was no reply to my many knocks. Finally, on my way back from dinner I saw her bike.

I walked myself straight to my room to think clearly. Should I just give her everything I had, and hope that somehow things would work out? Maybe it just might be okay to let my heart fly with her, soar with her for however long we had.

How unfussy life had seemed with her. How clean she was with her heart, her truth telling, simple and wise. She was mindful of my needs, tender with me. Even that stool had been a gesture of affection. I had known I was falling in love with her, maybe even when I first met her that late night when I arrived at the Institute. But I'd thought of Julia and how everything had unraveled.

I knew Ming was moving deeper into my heart, there was no doubt. Her gentle care for me seemed to be repairing my essential scaffolding, undone by Julia's infidelity. So I decided to go to her. I turned off the hot plate and went downstairs, hoping she would still see me.

"Ming?" I said, tapping on her door.

"Please come in," she said opening her door. "I am glad you came to me."

We sat wordlessly at her desk for an uncomfortable moment. I knitted my fingers together and cleared my throat.

"These days without you taught me how much I am coming to love you," I began. "When you were gone, I thought you had abandoned me and that made me terribly frightened and sad. But more importantly, I realized I want to let my heart be free to love again, to love you."

"You must be sure to me, Lu. Are you?"

"Every minute I am more sure."

She turned off the desk lamp, stood, and pulled me into her arms. The outside lights washed through the windows and the chalk blue walls paled; the cement floor was swabbed in silver.

"I do love you," I said. "And yet I am so afraid to really love you."

"I know," she whispered in my ear. "I love you and I am not."

She took my hand, leading me to her bed and we lay down next to each other. Then she took my hand, and placed it on her left breast.

I was on top of her, our blouses and bras long gone, kissing deeply. We found a rocking rhythm that was sublime. My hands moved again to her breasts and I felt her nipples begin to swell. I took her right nipple into my mouth and she moaned; I circled her swelling with my tongue as her body began to arc up, pushing her breast deeper into my mouth.

"Oh Lu, tonight I want everything with you," she gasped.

We quickly removed the rest of our clothing.

"I will get the warm water and soap and we can wash each other. Then I want my tongue on you. May I do that? Will you do that with me?"

"Oh god, yes. Absolutely."

She walked over to uncork the thermos, her nakedness dusted by the simple lumens of the outside lights, reaching in, defining her shape, and I was eager for her.

Now standing behind her, the length of our naked bodies touching for the first time, I said, "Ming, I want to sleep with you tonight, stay with you until morning,"

"Are you afraid?" she whispered, leaning back into me.

"Yes, I am still afraid," I said putting my arms around her. "But, right now, I am less afraid than I was several hours ago. If you will have me, I would love to wake up with you in the morning."

"Yes, I will have you."

I lay down on her bed and she was beside me, her right hand inside my right thigh, and she slid her hand higher. She gently pressed right and I opened to her. "I love you deep Lu, don't ever forget this. Now we will wash."

SNAKE FEET

蛇 脚

I knew that after writing these thirty new words seven more times I would have them nailed for Friday, our weekly quiz day. The words were getting harder, the sentences more complex and slippery. I was being introduced to four-character metaphors that conveyed paragraphs, panoramas of meanings.

For example, 摆龙门阵 literally means "to position dragons at a door or a gate for a short period of time." When I thought about it, dragons at a gate would be rackety and noisy, so the meaning was the chaos of a lot of people talking. The everyday word 老田 also means to gossip or to chat. It was the elevated expression that was graceful; it was the allusion to classical Chinese literature that gave the expression a resonance and breadth. I absorbed it all, and the dragons too. I frequently dreamt in Chinese and could even make decent puns and tell jokes.

Just as I had begun my 43rd round of writing, my door opened and there she was. I spun around to take her into my arms.

Kissing with her was always splendid and classy, but this

evening she was buzzing.

"What?" I asked, scooting the other chair to my desk and putting my cushion on the seat for her.

Sitting down, she played: "What, what?"

"You have an extra zing this evening. Did you find eggs on sale?"

"I have some news," she said laughing, taking my hand.

"Okay, let's hear it," I said, kissing her fingers.

Releasing my hand, she stood and twirled around behind me. Putting her arms around my neck and her lips to my ear she whispered, "No."

"No?"

"Nope," she teased as she spun back into her chair.

"I bet you want me to try and guess."

"You could try," she played. "But you're not that good."

"When will you tell me?"

"Oh, maybe soon."

"May I offer bribes?"

"You have to try to see," she said standing up again. She put her right hand on her hip and swung her left shoulder forward, flirting full and flashy.

Standing up in front of her, I slowly pulled her by her braids towards me until her lips were right next to mine.

"You won't stand a chance," I played back. And kissed her quick. We began hugging each other with increasing passion.

"Hold on here, little Missy," I said. "We either get naked right now or we go for a walk."

"Let's take a walk. You still have homework," she said, winking at me.

"Get your coat and I'll meet you at your door," I said.

I closed my character-writing practice book and capped my fountain pen. Whatever she might have up her sleeve, it must be a big deal. I had never seen her so animated and thrilled. I wondered how long she could hold out before she spilled her secret, or how long I could wait. I grabbed my coat, flicked off the light, and stood in the darkness for an attentive moment. My heart bloomed ever deeper for her.

When I joined her in the hall, her eyes held me with a fervor that matched my own. We walked out into the cold air, shivering a bit. It wasn't yet completely dark, but it was no longer day. We linked arms and snugged together as we fell into step.

Stepping over the bike-stopping pipe, a small gust of wind swirled dust, bits of paper, and a lone oil ration coupon. Ming stopped to pick up it up.

"Okay babycakes, I have a guess. You are now the chairwoman of the Communist Party."

Stuffing the coupon into her pocket, she said in Chinese: "Certainly not, I am not eighty years old."

We walked silently, arm in arm along the moonlit road that emptied onto a brighter street, on toward Wu Dao Kou. We saw straggling peasants sitting under dim electric lights strung on ropes. They hoped for last minute sales of their garlic, onions, eggs, potatoes, and peanuts.

Three up-turned oil drums had small fires glowing in their cut-out bellies, with a dozen or so roasting sweet potatoes on top. That delicious smell filled the night air and I offered a bribe.

"I will buy you a potato if you tell me your secret."

"Not enough. But I will eat one anyway."

"Oh you are going to be tough." I laughed and handed her a potato wrapped in the *Beijing Evening News*. We walked on, peeling the paper down as we ate.

Kicking a broken bottle to the side of the road, I offered another guess. "You bought a new car?" She just shook her head and clucked her tongue.

We silently checked the quality of the garlic a farmer was offering at his space on a long table. It was crudely cobbled together with bamboo poles and fraying ropes. Ming chose three garlic heads, paid the peasant his four *fen*, about two cents, and slipped them into the cloth shopping bag she always carried in her pocket. We moved on to the onions and potatoes.

The potatoes were well formed, the onions fragrant and fresh.

"Sweetcakes, let me pay for these."

"Your words," she laughed. "So different, so big in my heart. I like you calling me your cakes."

"If you tell me now, I will hold you all night."

"That bribe won't work. You'll hold me anyway."

"Then let's go get a couple of *shar bing*. Will that pry it out of you?"

"Nope."

Giggling, we strolled toward the open-air *shar bing* kitchen. I noticed there was more broken glass.

"Why are there so many broken bottles?"

"It is protesting. The people will often smash small bottles to protest against Deng Xiao Ping." Switching to Chinese, she explained: "His name, *Xiao Ping*, it means the Dawn of Peace. With different tones it can also mean small bottles."

"So, when the people get angry they protest by breaking little bottles?"

"Yes, that is it," she said kicking a shard to the side of the road.

I bought two *shar bing* also wrapped in the evening newspaper. We sat down on a bench under a camphor tree, shuffling our feet in the fallen leaves and drying berries, releasing the smell of dried rosemary. We looked at each other as we remembered washing each other's hands under a camphor tree many months ago; we shared a soft smile. Then we leaned forward to keep the grease off of our shoes and crunched into those delicious fried sandwiches.

"I need to go back and finish my homework," I told her as we took our last bites. "I will come to your room afterwards and wash you if you will tell me your secret."

"This comes almost close; you do this very well. So yes, you come to me when you finish."

I took her oily piece of paper, wadded it with mine and started for the nearby trash bin. She put her hand on my arm to hold me back.

"Now I want to tell."

I sat down again, turning toward her. She looked down and smiled, silently savoring her news. Then she slowly looked at me with a smile in the corner of her eye.

"My mother is coming to meet you," she said beaming.

A dizzying array of noisy dragons began forming up in my head. My mother, disparaging me at every turn: "You'll never amount to anything" was her frequent slice. Julia's mother had decided well before I met her that I wasn't good enough for her daughter. Once, she invited only Julia for a brunch, telling her she didn't want me there. Julia had told her we both would go or she wouldn't. Her mother's frozen smile, her frozen heart remained unchanged the entire time we were together. Would Ming's mother also keep me away with undefined hurdles, a finish line shifting with her whim, never quite achievable?

"I am looking forward to meeting her," I finally said. I considered pretending excitement, but gave that notion up quickly; Ming would know right away I was being disingenuous.

"What are you thinking?" she asked, gripping my wrist. "Your face looks sad."

"I really do want to meet her," I said, balling the newspapers tighter. "I'm just not sure she will like me, and maybe she will think I am not good enough for you."

I looked down to the oily ball in my hands, feeling old wounds gathering into those untidy folds, holding rejections that still remained too accessible.

"Many times you asked for the official permissions to go to my village, to meet my mother. Now, she is coming to you, and you are not happy." She shook her head. "Lu, you are a big goose."

She noticed that I was still not present with her.

"Calm your heart," she said. "Let's go home now." She slung the shopping bag over her shoulder and slid her other arm into mine, then she continued, "You will see, my mother will like you."

We walked quietly past the merchants who were finally packing up for the night, past the broken bottles and the aroma of roasting sweet potatoes, *shar bing* and peanuts which settled behind us.

"In ancient China," Ming began softly, "there were several people who competed in drawing a snake. One of them finished early, and added feet to the snake. So another one said, 'A snake doesn't have feet, why do you add them?'"

"I understand you," I said. "Don't make things worse than they appear."

MING'S MOTHER

明的母亲

"We need everything clean," Ming said handing me a dustpan. "We must clean the sheets, scrub the floor, and take away all the dust in this room."

"Why?"

"We are going to have a guest."

"Who's coming, the Empress of China?"

"No, my mother, she called to me this morning. She is ready to meet you."

I pulled her into my arms. "Finally, after three weeks she's coming."

"There is no time for hugging. She will be here Saturday morning."

"Babycakes, this is Wednesday afternoon," I said, still hugging her. "We have plenty of time to clean."

"We have other things to do. We must plan a feast for her, so we must shop."

"Okay then, let's clean until four o'clock," I said, sliding my hands down her arms to her fingers. "When they turn on the hot water, we'll do laundry and after that take our showers."

"Let's go," she said, also handing me a broom.

I started sweeping and began to panic. I could not let go of what might happen if her mom didn't like me. If she didn't like me, would she require that Ming leave me? Would Ming go along if her mom insisted? I didn't think so, but just considering it made me nervous. I was sweeping under the desk when Ming interrupted my pageant of fears.

"Stop, Lu. You are doing it wrong."

"There is no wrong way to use a broom, you just sweep."

"No, it is this," she said demonstrating short sweeps with her broom.

"Dammit, Ming, it doesn't matter. I'll just sweep."

She stamped her foot. "You are wrong, Lu. Do it right."

"Okay, okay." I was annoyed with her insistence on such a tiny thing. I wanted to tell her I was still anxious about her mother's arrival, but I didn't say anything, just used shorter sweeps.

To change the mood, I started to sing a Communist propaganda song, "Learn from Lei Feng." She joined in and we postured revolutionary poses, saluting with our brooms for dramatic effect. Lei Feng was probably a fictitious soldier in Mao's Revolutionary Army whose story was supposed to educate and serve the masses for the glory of the Revolution.

If we had found a thimbleful of dust, I would have been surprised; she was tidy with her room. Although there seemed to be nothing much to clean, I carried on beside her.

We washed the already clean sheets and towels; I helped her put them on the bamboo rack to dry and then left to do my homework. When I returned, she was cleaning the surfaces of her tea tins. Her diligence was endearing.

"Whew, I am tired," she said spinning a half circle and flopping onto her bed.

"You have done a lot of cleaning. We have just two more items to wash. I'll get the cloth, soap and warm water."

"Um hmm, let's do that."

Lying together, spent and quiet, I asked, "Do you want to invite others? Maybe Elizabeth and Guan?"

"No, she is coming just for you," she said rolling on top of me.

"This makes me nervous, you know." I wrapped my legs around her. "What if she doesn't like me or thinks I am not worthy of you?"

"She may treat you like a daughter from ancient times,maybe say things that you aren't used to hearing. She is old and maybe believes in ghosts, so don't listen to her when she makes no sense."

"Ming, if she doesn't like me, and tells you to leave me, would you do it?"

She took my face into both of her hands, looked me square in my eyes, and said, "Never." Then she started tickling me. "She will like you, Lu. No worry."

I laughed and pushed her hands away. "What shall we cook?"

"We'll make the *jiao zi*; knife cut noodles, even though this isn't New Year's time; sweet and sour soup; and apples. Oh, and a steamed fish."

"Sweetcakes, there will just be three of us."

"Every food is important: *jiao zi*, because they are like gold, so we eat for good wealth. Noodles because you will have a beginning with her. Soup for the mouth and stomach, and a fish because it will honor her."

I was silent, taken with her attention to details and their meaning. There was so much that was splendid about her: her tender manner, her respect of traditions and their discreet signals. I wanted to know all the mysteries that lived in her heart but right now, I just hoped to receive her mother's approval.

"What shall I call her?"

"She will tell you after she decides. You wait for her to say. If she says call me Lau Ming, this is good. If she says call me Ma,

70

this is best."

Suddenly I felt like I was being crushed under the weight of centuries. I was nervous I would make an unintentional mistake and ruin everything; or maybe I would stumble into an insult and not even know I had broken a custom and offended her.

"What time will she arrive?"

"I will go to the bus stop on my bike and pick her up. Maybe we will get back by almost twelve."

"Shall we shop for the pork, cabbage, apples and fish early Saturday morning?"

"Yes, but we go to Zhung Guan Cun, they have better."

"What about the fish there, do they have the freshest and the best? I could go to the Friendship Store and buy one."

"The village will be good enough," she said giving me a side-eye glance.

Just before we fell asleep, another cloud of anxiety scudded through. "Will she see me as just a foreigner, someone who comes from the West that was often disrespectful of China?"

"No, she will see past that. She has things you will have to look past too."

"What do you mean?"

"Her feet are bound."

I was surprised. I thought about her mom's feet. I knew something about the pain and disfigurement, which usually began around age four. The entire process took about two years at the end of which a girl's feet would be essentially dead, the girl unable to take a purposeful stride. I wondered if I might get to see firsthand what her feet looked like. I wondered if it would be okay to ask Ming if it would be acceptable to see her feet; maybe it would be a mistake to even bring it up. I decided not to say anything; it seemed too delicate, something to look beyond.

On Saturday we had a cup of tea and shared a bun before riding north just after dawn. We stopped at the first abundant display of vegetables and fruits, to buy eggs, tomatoes, long garlic sprouts, cabbage, and apples. I asked about the eggs and tomatoes; she told me they were for breakfast on Sunday.

"How long will your mom stay?"

"Until Sunday, maybe eleven o'clock. Be careful the eggs."

I hadn't realized I had whipped the shopping bag around for several full loops.

"I'm sorry, I'm antsy about your mom. What do I call her until she tells me what to call her?"

Looking at me from the corner of her eye, shaking her head, she said, "Quiet your heart. You can call her *lau nai*."

Okay, I thought, *I can do that. Lau nai* is a term of respect for an older woman.

"Now we need the fish. Do how I told you, Lu. Pick a good one."

Facing the big glass tank with dozens of swimming fish, I remembered what to ask the fishmonger. "Please give me a fat happy bass," I said in Chinese.

His eyebrows were raised the whole time he netted and bagged a gorgeous fish. He stammered the price, mystified by this foreign guest's specific request. His eyebrows were still up when I paid him and we walked away.

We laughed about him while we bought a lean slab of pork, still laughing on the way back to our bicycles, and all the way home. Every time I looked at her, she imitated his raised eyebrows.

We rode home at an easy pace, laughing, and discussing tasks and preparations. Cold showers were first, and then I would prepare the apples and vegetables, and chop the pork. Ming would gut the fish and put it in a pan of cold water until she and her mom returned.

As I went back to her room after my shower, she pulled me into her by my waist and gave me a big wet kiss.

"Whoa, do we have time for this?" I asked.

"No, we don't. I want you to think about this, not Ma. And

to remember she might say things you are not used to hearing. You must ignore these."

I returned to my room to do my homework after our tasks were finished. Memorization wasn't possible, so I practiced writing Monday's new vocabulary assignment. One idiom held my attention, *niao yu hua xiang*, "on a fine spring day." I certainly hoped it would be so.

I kept my eye on the clock. About a quarter to twelve, I took a deep breath and went outside; sitting on the front cement steps I fidgeted, waved to a pair of Palestinian classmates, and waited.

Around the corner and up to the building they rolled. Ming carefully braked. Her mom's face was soft and wrinkled, recalling the same golden beauty as Ming. Her hair, more silver than black, was pulled back into one long braid. She held me with her eyes, evaluating me.

I went up to her and took the large, heavy package from her lap, bowed slightly and said in Chinese: "*Lau nai*, I am honored to meet you."

"I am happy to meet you too," she said politely, without enthusiasm.

As Ming helped her off the bicycle, she looked at me top to bottom, adjusted her jacket, smoothed out a few wrinkles, then took my eyes hard for several long seconds. She said nothing more.

She looked to be about five foot three. Her jacket was gray and her trousers a darker gray; her tiny shoes were black with embroidered red and gold peonies. They looked new.

She leaned on Ming's arm, tottering slowly atop her little feet, moving down the hallway to Ming's room. I walked behind them carrying her package, my heart sinking, afraid I was not going to receive her benediction.

Ming pulled out a chair for her mom, and she sat down. She looked at me hard again; it seemed like an imperial examination.

I held my breath as Ming stood still, also holding hers. We waited while she picked unseen lint off her trousers, finishing her assessment.

Looking at me square in the eyes, she said to Ming "I want some tea." And then she cast her criticizing eye around Ming's room.

Ming and I both sagged; I wanted to run away.

"What do I call you?" Lau nai growled at me as she leaned back on the chair, and sighed from the trip and effort.

"Please, call me Lu."

"What kind of name is this?" she barked.

I felt like I had just been slammed against an ancient stone wall.

Ming jumped in, bowing with deference, explaining in Chinese that Louise had too many letters for her mouth, "so I made it shorter for me."

Lau nai guffawed, and scolded Ming for being lazy. I started to laugh but got the "don't laugh" look from Ming, and quickly stifled myself.

"Ming," Lau nai demanded. "Open the bag."

Inside was probably three pounds of freshly roasted peanuts that cradled five or six perfect cucumbers, Lychee nuts, several huge tomatoes, and a dozen eggs carefully wrapped in cotton batting. I was impressed that she had struggled with these gems for her daughter over what was surely a strenuous trip.

Ming handed her a cup of her best jasmine tea and thanked her several times. Then she moved one of the short stools under her mom's feet. Every chance I got I looked at her miniature shoes, trying to imagine her as a little girl, struggling through the pain of the binding process. I wished it were otherwise.

Ming moved the hot plate to the center of the room to keep the furniture from catching fire and plugged it in. When I slid the other short stool near the hot plate and sat down, I saw a dust bunny under the bed and laughed to myself. Ming put a large pot of water on the hot plate to boil.

First we would make the *jiao zi*. I rolled out the dough, Ming put the filling into the cut-out circles, and the three of us began to fold them. Her mom began to laugh.

"Lu," she said in Chinese. "You cannot fold these correctly. I think you must be stupid."

Ming bit her lip, squinched her eyes closed.

"It's okay, I know I'm not good at this," I said in English to Ming.

"You are right, my *jiao zi* are ugly," I told her in Chinese. She was right, but did she have to say it out loud?

Our cooking and eating continued, but she wasn't happy with the food. She told us everything was tasteless, and that Ming was a terrible cook. This disparaging talk carried on even with the final flourish of the fish. Ming was very good at steaming fish, and I thought she had surpassed her exceptional skills this evening.

Reverently, she served Ma the sweetest part of the fish, the middle, the ultimate sign of respect. Lau nai closed her eyes; we hoped, to savor her efforts. But it wasn't enough. She scolded Ming for giving her second-rate food and spit it on the floor.

When she told Ming she was a rotten daughter, my throat tightened and my teeth clenched. My hand instinctively moved to an old scar on my chest from one of my mother's belt buckle beatings. I had had enough. I stood up, ignored Ming's eye-full plea of *don't say anything*, and lambasted her mother.

"You are a mean old woman. You are harsh to your daughter and rude to me." My fists balled and my arm muscles grew taut. "Do you know how much effort we, she, put into your visit? You are ungrateful and undeserving."

Before I began to cry, I went out the door and closed it hard.

I stomped up the stairs. In the yellow-gray light of the outside lamps, I sat down on the edge of my bed, putting my head in my hands. Why was she so mean to Ming and to me? I was bruised by her insensitivities and everything that had happened, especially the strict manners and protocols. One thing I knew for sure: I had failed. I was exhausted by the unfamiliar dances and afraid of the fallout—what would happen between Ming and me now that I had bungled any chance of her mother's approval? Still angry, I slid into bed.

In the morning, I didn't want to go to Ming's room. I was afraid to face her after telling her mom off. I thought I should apologize, but I didn't know how or how it would be taken. It would be awkward and icy, but if I didn't go, I would fail Ming again.

At precisely nine, I knocked on the door. Ming opened it, took my arm, and aimed me to a stool. When I sat down, she handed me a bowl of rice covered with a tomato and egg dish.

We three sat awkwardly for a few long moments. Postures were shuffled, breaths were taken, and eyes darted. I was sure that whatever sliver of chance I had had to win her heart was gone now.

I could barely swallow and certainly not talk. Ming told me her mom had cooked the dish. Still not wanting to give up, I decided to try and secure a sliver of her favor. I would be extra respectful, and said in Chinese, "Lau nai, this dish is wonderful."

They both burst out laughing, laughing hard. I wasn't laughing; I wasn't in on the joke. And then I realized I was the joke.

"You just called her an ignorant sun hat." Grabbing her belly, gathering her breath, Ming said, "You used the wrong tone."

I surged to a deep red, wanting to get very small, run away, and hide. But the old woman was laughing, and everything around her softened: the air, her face, and our spirits.

Then she shook her head and said to Ming, "She is stupid. How can you want someone that stupid?" When she turned her gaze towards me, her laughter stopped. She stared at me and shook her head. The air thickened again.

I looked down into my bowl, sucking disappointment, and anger. I gave up. I was no longer going to try to win her heart. If this was the prize, I no longer wanted it.

"Ming, it's time for me to go," Lao nai said.

Ming, cringing a bit, tied up a small bundle of food for her to take home.

Lao nai steadied herself on Ming's arm, teetering down the hall on her tiny embroidered shoes. I carried the bundle, still fuming, walking behind them. And then I stood stiffly just behind her mom on the sidewalk while Ming went to get the bicycle.

Ming returned and settled Lao nai on the back of the bike and I placed the bundle on her lap. "Go," she told her daughter.

As Ming pedaled her away, she kept her eyes on me, eyes of sharp-edged steel. Even as the guards at the gate lifted the bike with her still on the back gently over the pipe barrier, she held me in her gaze. Then she was gone.

I went back to Ming's room to tidy up for her. I did the dishes, made the bed and wiped the surfaces clean. When I noticed the perfect white eggs in Ming's brown bowl, I began to cry.

There was so much to think about and try to understand. I plugged in the hot plate to warm the room and lay down on Ming's bed, sorting, making sense of the last day's events. I was miserable, certain Ming would never forgive me. I must have dozed off, because the next thing I knew she was sitting next to me, smiling.

"I didn't hear you come in," I said reaching up to caress her.

"I was quiet, I saw a chance to surprise you." Tapping my shoulder she said, "Let me lay next to you, I have much to say."

We wrapped ourselves together and she began. "My mother called me lazy, she called you stupid. She used harsh words for us like I said before. These are not the words she means. She is old, sometimes she still believes in ghosts. She thinks that if a ghost hears her say good things it will be jealous and take those things away."

"She made me mad when she criticized you about the food. I thought it was the best you had ever prepared."

"Same ghosts. She was afraid the ghosts would come and steal food."

"She didn't even like the fish belly," I said, fingering a few strands of her hair back into place. "This is all confusing. Has she ever offered you a compliment and waited to see if a ghost would show up?"

"Of course not, there are no ghosts. I think she knows this, but she is careful."

I was quiet for a moment, unsure. "I must have offended her deeply when I told her to stop being mean to us. I think I may have ruined any chance to have her like me."

"We talked this again going to the bus stop. She was surprised that you spoke so strong. Then she laughed, she said you are very American; I think she liked you more for that."

"And you?"

"I was angry at you and I was afraid too. I had never heard such words to my mother before. I didn't know what she would do." She paused for a second. "I thought first you should be quiet, not talk like that. Later I realized that is one way we are different. I am not so angry now, but I don't want that again."

I nodded my agreement. Then taking my hand and kissing my fingers, she said, "She left you a gift."

I looked and saw nothing.

Rising up on her left elbow she said, "It isn't in a box." Tracing my lips, looking deeply into my eyes, she continued, "She gave you a name, your Chinese name."

I was stunned. How could that be after what I said to her?

"We talked almost all night," she said pulling me closer. "Ma asked many more questions about you. This morning she told me that you deserved a better name than Lu. She used a sound from your American name, *Lin*—林. Next she gave you *Xiao*—晓, which means to deeply know important things; it also means to not know important things yet, like when the dawn comes and you can't see clear. Last is *Min*—敏. This means clever, very smart, and have good humor."

"So, sometimes I know what is deeply important and sometimes I can't see what's important yet."

"Yes, this is you," she said quietly, wiping a tear from my cheek. "My mother sees you."

The meaning of my new name, that my deeper self had been seen and revered, transported me to a new sense of well-being.

"Lin Xiao Min, I love you full, even when you are stupid and can't see clear."

"Even when I call your mother an ignorant sun hat?"

"Yes, even then."

HER LETTER

她的信

Ming burst into my room and laid several pieces of pink tissue paper on my vocabulary book.

They were about 2 inches by 4, and stamped with a red seal.

"What are these?" I asked, fingering the imprint of the official stamp of the Institute on the paper.

"They are movie tickets," she said. "I bought them for us. We go tonight after dinner. We can cook together."

"Knife-cut noodles and vegetables?" I asked stacking my books.

I opened my desk drawer for my wallet.

"No, Lu. No money," she said, taking my hand. "I want you to date with me."

"Sweetcakes, it would be my honor," I said standing and moving into her hug.

"I have another surprise. Elizabeth and Guan will meet us in the big hall for the movie. Tomorrow is Guan's birthday."

We swayed and squeezed and laughed, and then she whispered into my ear, "I have a bigger surprise."

"Oh dahling," I said, pretending a fainting spell and falling onto my bed, "Ah just couldn't stand another sa-prize."

Laughing, she landed on top of me and our kisses became more delicious and tender.

"Let's not cook," I suggested. "Let's just get some *shar bing* and then the movie."

"Yes, I like this," she said caressing my cheek with the back of her fingers.

"What movie is playing?"

"An American movie, from 1941. It's called *Sea Wolf.*"

She rolled herself on top of me and wrapped me tight with her arms and legs. "Lu, do you feel me strong on you? Do you feel my heart holding your heart strong too?"

"Yes, I do."

"Now I will say my surprise." She shifted a little to her right so we could look at each other. "I have a scholarship to study at Oxford in London for almost a year. I will leave in middle August and come back next year in June."

I looked away. My stomach roiled. I was so quick to feel her gone, an absence that wasn't yet real. Then my stomach began to shrivel. I wanted to disappear before this incredible hurt could go deeper.

She reached out and held my face, fixing my eyes with hers. "Lu, what's the matter? I thought you would be happy for me."

"I am happy for you but I am very sad for me. How long have you known about this?" I asked in a croaky voice.

"Maybe one hour. My master teacher called me to her office then I came for you."

She moved on top of me and wrapped me again with her arms and legs.

"Lu, aren't you the most happy for my chance? I can go to England," she whispered in my ear.

We were quiet for several minutes, hugging. I was holding her so she wouldn't vanish.

"Tomorrow I will take the bus to go to Ma and tell her. I will come back to you Sunday afternoon."

"Just call her. Please don't go," I said, now pulling her just a little closer.

"Sometimes the phone is broken. If it works, I would have to leave a message for her with the cadre. This is not his business, so I must go to her. C'mon Lu," she said as we sat on the edge of the bed. "Let's go to Wu Dao Kou."

"I just can't go with you now," I said. My heart felt like crushed rock. "I need to be alone for a little while, maybe an hour."

"If I could take out all that pain in your heart, I would," she said putting her arm firmly around my waist, kissing my cheek. "Remember your name now, Lu."

I knew what she meant, to be the one who sees clearly in the dawn, not deceived by shadows. I could feel her from the inside of my heart out. Every time we came to my places of unease, she graced me with her patience.

She stood up and took my hands. "I know my chance to go out is hard for you, Lu. Now you must believe my deepest heart for you. Even if I am far from you, I will still love you. And I will come back for you."

"Please, Ming," I said, my shoulders slumping, tears welling. "Just go."

She opened my door and turned around, maybe to say something more; instead, she quietly closed my door and left.

I took the time to gather myself. Of course, this was a great honor for her and she was rightly excited and proud of the recognition, but I didn't want her to go. I couldn't imagine life here without her. And what if she found another to love in the excitement of London, someone far more worthy of her than me?

Then I became angry; I wanted to yell at her for leaving me. The old cluster of Julia's betrayal and abandonment surfaced as I curled into a ball and let the tears come from deep, deep inside where fear growls and guts twist. When I stopped sobbing, I felt the clutch of my monsters loosening; my parade of ogres was now retreating. It would take time for me to process this, and I knew I needed to pretend that all was well for her sake. After I washed my face, I got my coat and my shopping bag. I locked my door and went to her.

Standing outside her door, reticent from having dismissed her, I hoped I hadn't hurt her. I would apologize right away.

I knocked.

"Jin lai," she said

I stood before her, uncomfortable, and stammered my apology.

"Lu," she said, "I know your heart. Come to me now so I can hug you."

Our hug was relieving. I could feel my heart relax into her care.

"I can feel you are better now," she said. "Let's go."

She was lambent as we stepped into the late afternoon, while I felt gray; not bleak gray, but the way light scissoring onto a black rock might lighten its presence. She slid her arm through mine and we walked together at a pace that nearly matched.

"Do Elizabeth and Guan know your news?" I asked, stopping at an apple vendor. "Let's get some of these to serve with tea after the movie," I said.

"No, I only talk to you," she said handing me five fragrant apples. "I will tell them tonight."

She paid the peasant, and I slipped the apples into my bag.

We walked to the stand selling *shar bing* and I held myself back from bursting into tears. I would miss her terribly when she was gone, miss the way she made even the simplest things feel elegant. She handed me a sandwich and we sat down on a bench.

"Ming, I have an idea. Would you like it if I came to visit you during my summer vacation?"

She tilted her head and smiled at me. "Oh yes, very much,"

she said. "I wanted to ask this, but I know your money is small, so I was shy."

We were both quiet, eating and sharing tiny glances as the possibilities of being together in London began to take hold. But I still lurked in the gloom of her upcoming absence.

We walked home the long way. I could envision her feeling the exuberance of living in a new city, and us being together outside of China. She said she'd be my tour guide when I arrived.

"Ming," I started to say when a careless bike rider ran into my left arm.

"Hey you, that hurt," I yelled in Chinese.

He turned half around and mouthed an apology. "Be careful, dammit," I yelled louder.

Ming looked at me and I knew I had gone too far. My outsized response was aimed at her, not him.

Rubbing my arm, I let out a big breath. "I am angry with you for leaving me here. I'm trying really hard to be happy for you, but I'm not yet."

"Then don't come to London to me," she said clenching her teeth. "I don't want you there."

"Oh, is that so? All right fine, I won't. See if I care."

"Humph," she growled, putting space between us.

Our footsteps became little stomps. We each walked faster. I wanted to shed her nearness, to get away and be alone. What was happening to me? To us?

As we neared our building, a taxi pulled up near the front door and Elizabeth and Guan got out. We looked at each other with surprise since we expected to see them later. *Oh shit*, I thought. I had been counting on a little time to gather myself before the movie; now how the hell was I going to pretend nothing had happened?

Ming called out something in the Beijing dialect and Guan turned around laughing. "What did you say just now?" I asked as the four of us joined up.

"I asked her what are you two peasants doing in a fancy car?"

We all laughed as we walked into Ming's room, but it was funnier to Ming and Guan.

Elizabeth put a large plastic bag on Ming's desk and pulled it down like she was rolling a sock down a leg. We watched expectantly.

"Ta da, it's an apple pie," she announced. "I baked it this afternoon for my love's birthday."

"And to celebrate our movie date," Guan said.

"Oh my god, it looks wonderful. And look at that, a lattice crust," I said. "I so envy you, having an oven."

Ming started to laugh and began telling the story of when I tried to bake a cake. I wasn't sure if she was using the cake story to poke me with her anger.

"I got a terra cotta flower pot," I picked up her recounting. "Then inverted it over my hot plate. Hell, I didn't know the temperature without a thermometer, so by gosh and by golly, I plugged and unplugged the hole with an aluminum wad until I thought it was done."

"It was burnt," Ming finished the story, laughing harder. "But the middle didn't cook at all." She flashed me a dagger of a look unseen by the others. "It was terrible."

It hurt, but I pretended that it didn't.

"We threw most of it away, but I've gotten pretty good with potatoes."

"Wow, Lu, a master chef. Potatoes even. Good on ya."

"Stop," I said poking Elizabeth in the ribs. "Let's see you try to bake a cake with a flower pot."

The conversation quieted about then, as though everyone knew there was something to be said.

"I have something to tell," Ming said.

"Well, out with it, woman," said Elizabeth.

"I am going to London for a year to study at Oxford for English."

There were *oh*'s and *ah*'s and congratulations from all. Ming beamed. Guan hugged her, then Elizabeth. She leaned back into me and I put my hands on her shoulders.

Cheers, well wishes and questions continued for several minutes while I got plates and utensils. I handed Elizabeth the knife and she took aim at the pie.

"Here's to our newest world traveler, and to the second most wonderful woman in the world," she said waving the knife in the air.

"She is such a talker," Guan said taking the knife, then slicing and serving the pie.

It was delicious. The cinnamon was perfectly balanced and the crust flaky. And I envied her her oven even more.

"Oh, we have to go now to the movie," Ming said looking at her watch. "Let's go."

A few minutes into the half-mile walk to the auditorium, Guan and Ming walked side by side and Elizabeth and I fell into step behind them. "Are you and Ming okay?" Elizabeth asked.

"No, we're really not. We had a fight earlier, and it's not finished. I'm mad at her for leaving me here. I'm trying to maintain a good face, but it hurts like hell."

"You're a better woman than me, I would be throwing dishes."

"Don't think I haven't thought of that. I want to throw baseballs through windows and yell loud enough to scare the bacon out of pigs. I wanted to go see her at the summer break, but now she doesn't want me to come."

As we got closer to the auditorium, there were many more people walking along the road. Soon the way bustled with excited people, laughter, and noisy conversations. Young men, maybe sons, balanced their elders on their bicycles. Mothers carried toddlers, lovers and friends walked arm in arm, and everyone seemed to be carrying bags of food. It became apparent that this was a major event for our work unit, as hundreds were streaming in to see this old American movie, all for six fen, about three cents.

"Listen Lu, come to my place for breakfast tomorrow morning."

"Love to. Ten?"

"You got it, mate."

We got chairs in the fifth row, squeaky metal chairs that were a little lopsided. There must have been three hundred or more people in that auditorium, talking, sharing food and even rearranging their chairs into semicircles.

I ducked under the noise and shifted a bit closer to Ming. She did not move to me. Looking straight ahead at the blank screen I said softly, "Ming, I…"

"Shhh," she said, also staring ahead.

I think she said something else, but I wasn't sure what because the movie started. The sound was loud and boomy from cheap speakers; the dialog was a half a second out of sync and the Chinese subtitles flashed too quickly to read. But worse, the audience talked louder and continued to eat. I smelled garlic and heard complaints about daughters-in-law, the price of cooking oil, and bosses; and more potato recipes. There was nothing I could do about the boisterous crowd, nothing about the lousy movie and nothing about Ming leaving.

Later we stood outside our building with Elizabeth and Guan chatting until their taxi arrived. When they left, we stood awkwardly in the dim yellow light of the lamppost. I wanted to say something, to try to fix this scuffle before it festered, but I didn't know what to say. I took her arm and walked us to her room.

"Lu," she said unlocking her door. "I don't want you to be with me tonight. I need time to think this."

"Okay," I said, feeling her rejection claw deep as she closed her door.

The next morning Elizabeth met me on the restaurant's front porch. "If you don't mind," she said, "let's eat here. I am flying to Japan early this afternoon. Since it's about four hours away, I'm going to stay overnight and be back tomorrow." She chose a table near a window with a garden view.

"Ranch business?" I asked placing my cloth napkin on my lap.

"No, I broke my bloody siphon coffee brewer. I'm going to the Hario store to get a replacement, but mostly to eat some better food." The waiter handed us menus and left, and she continued. "I just got a parcel of gorgeous Kona coffee and splat, I broke the goddamn bottom glass. Here's a pound of Kona for you too."

"Wow, thank you so much. This is really nice of you and just in time too, my care package from my friends back home is nearly gone. Elizabeth, order whatever you want," I said. "The check's mine today."

"Thanks, Lu," she giggled.

The waiter took our order of eggs, potatoes, tomatoes and toast. And sausage. Elizabeth suggested we order it just to see what would arrive.

"Lu, when you and Ming are in London, just keep on going. Take her to the States, take her to LA or New York, and live together happily ever after."

"Now you're a romantic?" I looked at her and saw her brow furrow.

"Listen, Beijing is not a place to live for a long time. It'll grind you down and Communist policies aren't reliable." She paused a moment. "Political situations could change in an instant in this bloody country. I got here in late August of '76. One month later Mao died. One month after that his wife and three others were given the blame for the whole damn Cultural Revolution and put on trial."

Our breakfasts were placed before us and as soon as the

waiter left, we started laughing. The sausage, it turned out, was a red-cooked chicken breast.

"Do you want to live with a cement floor and a hot plate, and sleep with Ming on that crappy bed for years to come?"

"It does sound dire, doesn't it?" I said, pushing the chicken to the side.

"No shit, Lu. Listen mate, if you two decide to go to the States, I'll give you both the airfare. A lovely parting gift."

"Listen buddy," I said. "This may be a bigger fight than I thought. She left me at her door last night. No kiss, no hug. Said she wanted to be alone, I'm not sure we will get through this."

We stopped talking while the waiter set two cups of coffee in front of us.

"And, I don't know about taking her to the States. How would I take care of her and me too? She could get a job as a teacher, but she'd have to get a credential first, and even then, lesbians are not very welcome as teachers in California right now."

Elizabeth just listened, stirring a spoonful of sugar into her coffee cup.

"What about my plan to become a translator at the UN? I'd have to leave the Institute without my certificate. I don't know what to do, Elizabeth, I truly don't."

"Are you finished now? Any more reasons to not do what you really want, what she really wants? Lu, you're not thinking right. Just ask her to go with you. She loves you more than you see, she'll go anywhere to be with you."

I waved the waiter over and asked for coffee refills and the check.

"You know, I've dreamt about asking her to come with me, but sometimes I feel like I don't deserve her."

"Christ," she said, slamming the table with her hand. The silverware, cups, shakers and sugar bowl jumped up; people turned their heads. "Lu, goddammit," she said a little more quietly. "You do deserve her and she deserves you. Sometimes Lu, you are so goddamn dense."

She was right, and I knew it. Her perceptions were spot-on. She sat back sipping her coffee and I silently finished my breakfast and thought about what Ming had said about London.

"I'd love to stay here all day and solve your problems, mate, but I have to be on my way," she said after a while. I put the money on top of the bill and we left, linking arms, as we walked to the bike rack.

"Lu, first you've gotta fix the fight. Apologize deeply and sincerely, remind her that you're trying your best, then ask her on a date to the Golden Panda restaurant."

"I like that idea," I said unlocking my bike and pulling it from the rack. I smiled. I felt better. "All right, I will. I'll ask her on a date to that restaurant. And maybe to a hotel too, just to practice being bourgeois."

"You're something else, Lu." Elizabeth laughed, then hugged my shoulder and swatted me on my butt as I rode off.

I joined the flow of other bike riders and thought to myself, *now I may have a delightful surprise for Ming*. I was happy. Not delirious, but a calm happy, the kind that comes with having a plan of contrition and a notion of the future.

TALL NAILS

高钉子

"I found the note you secretly put in my pocket this morning," Ming said. "Yes, let's walk, then you ask me."

We sometimes took a walk after supper, but this time I wanted to make sure we did. There was still unease between us, even after much talking and struggle for the last several weeks. If we could settle things a bit more, then I would ask her to an elegant dinner date and begin the conversation of us being together forever.

The path was icy, hiding spots of hazard, so we stepped with care. The early evening winter light edged toward dusty yellow. That afternoon the winds from the Gobi Desert had ripped through Beijing, leaving ridges of wind-blown snow on the hedge tops. I could still see their green in the remaining light; those tiny drumlins held that light too, like floating goose bumps.

It began to snow again; that immense silence, that weight of air summoning soundless vespers. Several snowflakes came to rest on Ming's hair, and I bent slightly to her and kissed them off. When she looked up at me, her eyes catching the last light of sunset, she pulled me closer to her and smiled again as we continued to walk.

"Look," I said, pointing with my chin. A student's forgotten trousers had frozen on the clothesline and someone else had unpinned them and set them on the ground. Three pair of pants, freestanding, upright, waiting for legs; like soldiers, guarding nothing.

The weak bulbs from the street lamps elbowed the remaining light left by the now gone sun. As we continued walking east, the distance between the lamps grew until there were pockets of darkness. I had been thinking about Elizabeth's suggestion to take Ming to the States after London. I had spoken to Alice, my friend at my embassy, about visas and she assured me it could be done, although with some difficulty. Now, after weeks of thought, I had found the courage to ask her to come with me.

She stopped us in an island of inky dark, pulled my face to hers and kissed me. There was a fast moment when the cold on our lips vanished and our heat took its place.

We walked on in silence for another half mile, then sat down on a bench beneath a statue of Chairman Mao—the same statue that was positioned at every university—with his right arm perpetually raised, pointing east. Snow had collected between his stony fingers.

"Now you ask me," she said snuggling closer.

"I want to ask you out on a date."

"Why are you whispering?" she asked.

"Because the snowfall is so quiet, I don't want to interrupt."

"We just had a date," she said quietly, turning slightly toward me. "We saw a movie, did you forget?"

"We saw a movie with hundreds of other people who talked the whole time, and we sat on noisy metal chairs."

"So?"

"I mean something fancy," I said, sliding even closer to her.

"Tell me this date you want to take me to," she said.

"Well, you did take me to the movie, we have gone on a picnic, and we have gone shopping for a fish. I want us to go somewhere great, do something extravagant, really special."

I cleared my throat.

"I want to take you to the Golden Panda restaurant. Elizabeth told me the menu is exquisite."

"They ask too much money for food," she said in Chinese.

"Don't worry about the price, I am inviting you," I replied in Chinese. "And we will go by taxi," I said, switching to English. "We will sit in the back and do secret things when the driver isn't looking."

I thought she was warming to my idea since she was quiet; I thought she was thinking about how much fun it would be.

"And after dinner I will take you to the Great Wall Hotel," I said growing bolder. "I'll get us a room on the top floor, facing west. We can take a long shower together and sleep in a big bed." I was on fire now, thinking of all the wonderful things we could do together.

"And then in the morning we'll order—"

"Lu," she interrupted sharply, "I will not go."

She stood up quickly and started walking away.

What had just happened? What had I done? My heart froze and it wasn't the weather. Maybe she was still angry about our dustup concerning her going to Oxford. I sat there for a few tense moments watching her walk away, wondering what I had done now.

"Wait. Stop. You sounded angry with me," I said catching up with her.

"Yes, angry," she said. "You, a little, other things more."

"Why with me?"

"You because you made me think things. No more talking now. Let's go," she said in Chinese, gripping my sleeve as we began walking home.

The moon was full, the light sharp with ice. We could see the slippery spots on the path now and carefully walked around them. I wanted to know what had upset her. I should wait for her to tell me; I knew that. I ignored my advice.

"What happened back there?"

She stopped walking and stamped her foot all in the same motion. Her face pulled taut, her mouth drawn.

"I will talk when I have my words," she said through tightened lips. "You know this."

"I do know, dammit. I just get so nervous sometimes while you find your words." I was going to say more, defend and explain myself, when tears pearled in her eyes.

"Ah jeez Ming, don't cry," I said taking her arm, pulling her close to me.

She looked down, started walking again, and then said, "We will talk in my room. My words are close."

We walked the last quarter-mile more briskly. In that thick quiet, I silently berated myself for asking her to talk before she was ready.

We stopped just inside the front double doors of our building. There was an uncertain moment. She shifted her weight from her left foot to her right, and then softly asked, "Will you come to me now, stay the night with me?"

"You know I will. I'll get my best tea for you, I'll be right down."

She had lit three candles and the hot plate was a warm distance away from her desk. She poured water into her aluminum pot, set it on the hot plate, then sat down at her desk.

While she prepared the water, I put several practiced pinches of long jing tea into her porcelain cups, set them on the desktop, and sat down across from her. This time, I waited for her to speak.

She held me with her eyes for a moment, touched my face, then looked down to her hands.

"There are places that I am not allowed to go to in my own country."

"Like where?"

"Foreign embassies, the Friendship Store, hotels for foreigners, places like that."

"I can understand foreign embassies, but why not hotels? You could never go?"

"I could go to the hotel, but I would have to get a permit from the president of this Institute. I could also go to the Golden Panda restaurant with you, but I would need a permission for that too."

"Well, okay then, ask for the permits." I brightened.

"She would ask why I want to go to places only for foreigners, and what would I say?"

"You could tell her we want to eat really good food and then fuck our brains out."

"No joking now, you don't understand." She shifted on her chair, facing me full. "The reason is to keep Chinese people and foreign people apart. The government does it with privileges to you. If we try to have these luxuries, we will stick up like a tall nail. Tall nails are always pounded down."

She stood up and walked to the window. I watched her stand there, her back to me, silent. She turned around and leaned on the useless radiator. "Before I can go out to England, the government police will look at my history."

"Why, what will they be looking for?"

"To see if I am a moral citizen," she said compacting her hands into a ball, tightening them at her waist. "There are things that you don't know," she said. "We haven't talked them yet."

She got the teapot and poured boiling water into the teacups that I held up for her, and then she sat down at the desk again and took my hand.

She played with two of my fingers for a second, and took a deep breath. "When the Cultural Revolution reached my school

95

in 1966 I was thirteen. We were young and stupid, we didn't know right from wrong. We all wanted to join the Red Guards because nobody wanted to be backward or counter-revolutionary. Some of my classmates went to *Tian An Men* to see Chairman Mao, and when they came back we were told to attack the "Four Olds," old ideas, culture, manners and customs. We went like a mob to our school and found an unpopular teacher to denounce. One of the boys ripped his shirt and shoes off, another made him kneel and hit his feet many times with a brick."

Her face sagged into her hands. I reached out to her arm and waited.

"I slapped that teacher's face." She bit her lip. "He looked up into my eyes and I could see I had hurt him. His eyes had questions. I was afraid, but I couldn't show this, so I spit in his face, cursed him and slapped him again. I didn't want to, but I had to or the others might think I was a capitalist roader and my family might be hurt."

I was stunned. It didn't make sense to me that this woman I knew as kindhearted would participate in this chaos. Before I came to Beijing, I had thought of the Red Guards as a gang of young men, like Boy Scouts gone a little wild. But I had since come to know that the Red Guards had become brutal as they reached their full might, destroying many of China's historical buildings and temples; families and souls were trampled in their zeal for Mao's mandate of purification.

"What happened after that?" I asked carefully.

"Nothing else. My body was shaking too much." She took a sip of tea. "Later in the week, many of my classmates got into army trucks to go to the city to attack bourgeois people. I pretended to have my period, so I didn't go. When they came back there were many stories about stealing things and breaking people's bones."

"Did you ever see the teacher afterward?"

"I stayed away from him, I walked out of my way to avoid

his home." She took a deep breath. "Before I left for college, I went to apologize to him but I learned that he had died."

Tears began to stream down her face and I wiped them with my fingers.

"He was sent to the countryside after we attacked him and his family was shunned for being capitalist roaders. Two years later he drank poison and killed himself."

"That's really awful, but I don't see how that will keep you from going to London. Many young people were misguided during those times, maybe did things they wouldn't do now."

"Lu, to this day that is a stone in my heart."

"I think that teacher would have accepted your apology, forgiven you."

"But Lu, this thing can make me a tall nail. Maybe I won't get to go out of China. This is also why I won't go to your date. It would put notice on me." She sighed deeply, and looked at me. "I think you shouldn't try anymore for the travel permit to go to my village. Maybe too much attention." Her forehead wrinkled deep worry.

"Okay, I won't."

I stood up and she slipped into my arms. I held her close, wondering about what other tragedies she had yet to talk about. More, I now understood why she had been upset earlier. My accumulating recognitions about this sinister underbelly of China and capricious government policies began to produce a penetrating network of small white ice needles on my heart. I hugged her tighter, wanting so much to halt the spread of that chill.

"You are squeezing my bones," she said.

"Ming, I don't want you to be a tall nail," I said. "Your opportunity to be in London is too important."

"We won't think this anymore now, Lu. We can think tomorrow." Pulling my earlobe with her lips, she whispered, "Let's prepare for sleep."

She unplugged the hot plate and parked it safely next to the hopeless radiator. I got a pan, poured warm water into it, and got the soap and a cloth.

She blew out the candles save one, and we undressed each other with care and kisses. Then we washed each other, that sensuous, particular ritual of our own attention.

As we lay together, quietly catching our breath, she whispered, "I really do want to go on your date with you." She slid onto my belly and lay on top of me. "Someday we will do, just do, decadent, bourgeois, Western things together." She kissed my eyes closed and said in Chinese, "I want to do everything with you."

She had told me a dark secret and I could feel her vibrating with uncertainty. I wanted to offer some comfort, a distraction.

"Sweetcakes, I have another idea."

"Oh my, what now?" she played. "We ride horses to Mongolia?"

"Oh, I like that, shall we?"

"Of course not," she said. "Tell me your mind."

"How about we invent a date we can go on, something that doesn't involve politics or compromises?"

She snuggled into my right side as she thought it over. "Yes, I want this." She wiggled even closer.

"How about this, let's take one week and gather surprises for each other. We can make things, or borrow, or buy, or cook things. Whatever we want to do for each other."

"Oh Lu, I like this. When do we date?"

"How about next Saturday at eight o'clock in your room?"

"Two weeks is better," she said.

"Done. We will make our own date."

When we awoke the next morning, we saw that the snowfall had stopped.

Frost remained.

OUR DATE

定 婚

Quietly, over the next two weeks, a truth emerged, the one salient and essential fact: she loved me. It was there in her eyes, in the ordinary moments of a day. In her manner of kindness and humor that held me cherished. As long as I could remember that, keep my feet under me and not unnerve myself with old scars and nightmares, I believed her. I trusted her.

I considered the issues of upheaval and relocation for both of us. I also ping-ponged myself with secondary and useless questions. I agreed with my best friend, Elizabeth: our future was in the States, not China.

Oh, how far I had come since I had arrived here with my shattered heart. I found myself wanting to make a long life with this sensitive, passionate woman. I was sure she would want to come with me and I planned on asking her in a few hours, at just the right time. I checked the green plastic clock on my bookcase. It was nearly eight in the evening and in a few minutes we would have our date. I put two jars of yogurt, spoons, and a hyacinth bulb into my green satchel, then opened my desk drawer for a final gift: a Chinese counterfeit of Camay. The shape and color were correct and the fragrance nearly so, but this soap had accidentally been rechristened *Comay*. I stuffed it into my bag and hurried down to Ming's room.

When I opened her door, her room was an inexplicable mess. The bed was unmade, her socks and underwear were hanging wet on the bamboo rod, and dirty pots and plates sat on too many surfaces. I wondered if the first part of our date would include housekeeping activities.

"Are you ready for our date?"

"Yes, I am."

"But, Ming, your room is a mess." I was disappointed, annoyed really, that there would be housework to do before we could begin our festivities.

She started to giggle.

"I have played a good joke on you. Remember when we agreed we could borrow something?" she asked, tugging my earlobe with her lips. "We will go to what I borrowed."

"One minute," she said, as she opened her wardrobe drawer and put a bag of peanuts into a pillowcase. "Okay, I am ready. Let's go to my bicycle. I will be our taxi. You will sit behind me and hold on to me."

After a shaky start, and nearly dumping me off, she rode with confidence and increasing speed into the dark night. My left hand held the pillowcase and my satchel rested in my lap. With my right arm, I held her around her waist, then slowly inched my hand under her sweater to her left breast. She swatted it down and then rang the bicycle bell three times, at no one, probably me. I held her tight and squeezed her waist three times responding to her bell ringing. Laying the right side of my face on her back, I could feel her muscles powering the bicycle. I closed my eyes and savored this humble sweetness. I don't think I had ever gone on a date on the back of a bicycle. With a woman by my side, tacking a Chrysler New Yorker down an LA freeway for sure, but not like this, slow and simple. The cool night air hinted roasting sweet potatoes as it eddied around her body to mine.

Maybe twenty minutes later she slowed, which signaled my dismount. We parked the bike, and walked into a five-story building that was somewhat familiar. She led us up three flights of chipped cement stairs; each landing was lit by a single naked lightbulb that barely illuminated high stacks of white cabbages belonging to the residents of each floor. As she dug the key out of her pocket, I remembered that this was where her friends Hu and Qin lived. Spending the evening with them was not what I had in mind.

"Close your eyes, Lu," she said unlocking the door, "I have a date surprise. No peeping," she said, guiding me into the room. She took my coat and satchel and tossed them somewhere; I heard them land with a thud. Then I heard her take her coat off. "Still no peeping, Lu," she said.

"Hurry up, I want to see what this is all about." I heard her plug in the hot plate and strike a match. I just barely squinted one eye open. I could see her taking her blouse off.

She took my arm and said, "Two more steps. Stop here. Now, open your eyes."

Before us was a double bed. The single candle lit the peacock blue cover to luminescence, and Ming, to a warm gold. I looked at her and saw her blush.

"This is absolutely spectacular," I said, falling with her onto the bed. "How did you manage this?"

"They went to his village to visit his family," she said as we wiggled and rolled around on the huge bed. "Hu said I could use their room until Sunday evening. I came here early to prepare for us."

She rolled herself on top of me and pinned my arms above my head and kissed me with tongue. "Lu," she growled, "I want to fuck your brains out."

I laughed out loud at her use of slang.

"Did I use it wrong?"

"No, it was perfect."

We removed our clothes. Quickly.

She caressed my breasts and took my nipples into her mouth, tugging each with her lips. She stroked me with her hands and slowly kissed her way down my body. Just before she opened my legs she said, "Now I will wash you."

I watched her walk across the room in the light of the single candle and the glow of the hot plate coils. While she poured hot water into a pan, I looked around the room and saw a long elm-wood dresser and a small table with two chairs under one of the east windows. Then I noticed that she had arranged some tender gestures. On the right nightstand sat a new cloth, two apples and a pear in the white bowl from her room. On the left stand stood a vase of wildflowers and the single candle she had lit.

"I see that you bought a new cloth." Then I remembered the Comay. "Wait, Sweetcakes, I got us a new bar of soap," I said, jumping up and finding my satchel. She laughed and commented about how we knew each other so well. I returned with the soap and she turned off the hot plate and blew out the candle.

"Tonight," she said sitting on my belly, "everything is for you. This my biggest date gift to you."

I reached up and caressed her breasts. Our eyes held each other ever deeper. She slowly lowered herself down onto me. We both sighed and quieted briefly as we savored that sensation that always seemed so new.

"Lu, I want all of you, everything that we know to do. Open to me now so I can touch you."

We were ferocious for each other. Together we growled to landscapes of wild light, of deeper, touching with remembering tongues and practiced fingers, as if we could make everything possible and last forever. We fell, exhausted, sweat and breath mingled with tears, and wet. We pulled each other into a deep hug releasing the final spasms of orgasm. There was a shift to a deeper, wider place than we had known before. We both felt it; our bodies knew it.

I ran my fingers in her hair, caressing her cheek when a tiny despair arrived. "It will be many months that I will live here without you. How will I do that?"

"It will be a short time," she said snuggling to find her fit. "We will write every day."

"My arms aren't long enough to reach you in London from here," I said, adjusting to her.

"I will ask Tian to take care of you."

"Will she kiss me goodnight too?"

"I forbid that," she said.

"I will miss you more than I can say, you know," I said, kissing her fingers.

"I will miss you so much too. But we will be together in London, it won't be too long."

"Several months isn't that long, I guess," I said, putting her hand on my heart. "But it will feel like four thousand years."

"And then you will come back to Beijing without me," she said, putting her head on my chest.

Here it was, the chance I had hoped for. For a short moment I withdrew my attention from her, to be totally alone with this. I had to steady myself. But in that instant, I lost my nerve. I would just become undone if she said no; I might not survive in one piece.

"I'll just wait for you here," I said in a tiny voice, beating myself up for not asking her. "I will come to the train station and bring you home when you come back to Beijing."

She moved her head from my chest to the pillow next to mine. "Are you okay? Your voice was different."

"Yeah, yeah," I fibbed. "I'm okay. I was thinking about being here without you twice."

"Lu, the time will go fast," she said holding my face. "Kiss me goodnight, let's sleep now."

I was awake before her. It was just dawn, and blue-mauve light angled its fingers through the east windows, through the curtain cracks, and inched onto her, making lucid her golden beauty. I rested my head on my arm, watching her sleep. What an enormous undertaking it would be to get us to the States. I felt the heft of the hundreds of tiny decisions we'd have to make, and the leaps we would need to make for each other. I imagined what we might be like when we were both ninety, having grown old together. And I hoped, so deeply hoped, that she would come with me. I promised myself I would ask her first thing. When she awoke, she sleepily pulled me closer.

"How are your brains, Lu?" she whispered. She began tickling me and we rolled over each other and giggled and squiggled with all the room in the bed.

"About as fucked as yours, my dear cakes."

"Let's get up," she hooted, "I need the bathroom. You make me laugh too hard."

When we returned and dressed, I helped her spread some newspapers onto the table, then arranged two plates, paring knives and two spoons and we sat down across from each other.

"I want to give you another date gift now," I said, retrieving my satchel, pulling out the bulb wrapped in the *People's Daily*. As I handed it to her, I kissed her forehead. "It is a hyacinth bulb, purple, I was promised. When it blooms to its full beauty, it will only be second to you."

"Lu, this will be beautiful. I know this flower; it smells very sweet. We can go together to the Temple of Heaven and get a good pot."

"Okay, we'll have another date."

"Yes," she said, "we will do this."

I cracked several handfuls of peanuts open for us while she peeled an apple. I gathered my courage as she spun the red skin down.

"Ming, I want to ask you something."

"Of course," she said.

"You don't have to answer now. I just want us to talk it through, take all the time you need." I took a deep breath. "Come with me to America after we meet in London."

She looked at me, blank, and said nothing. I could barely breathe. She continued her long silence until I thought I must surely burst.

The spiraled apple skin fell to the table, while the knife and the naked apple remained poised in her hands. Laying them down, she looked at me square.

"Have you been thinking this all week?"

"Longer than that to be honest. Before I could ask you I had to be sure, so I could make a full, clean promise to you."

"Lu, I need more thinking. Maybe I won't be able to see Ma again."

I felt her attention leave, saw her face shift to other horizons. I wanted her to say, just say yes, and I had to honor my promise to give her the time she needed to think things through. But how long could I stand not knowing?

"Lu, I don't know. I don't know how to choose. Maybe this is too big for me."

I launched into all the details I had worked out. We would live in LA, maybe a little place in Silver Lake. I could ask friends for some of their unused furniture and we would get jobs. I might put in an application to the *Los Angeles Times*; I had often thought of working there. Or, I considered further, maybe Kaiser Permanente would be hiring. Then we'd find a job for Ming. I was nearly sure that now that my personal hurdle had been successfully jumped, we would be on our way soon enough.

She was silent, looking down at the delicately resting apple peel. "Lu, I need to think this."

"How much time do you need? I mean, don't you know right now? Just say yes."

"I ask you to let me think and you push on me. So no, Lu, I won't go with you."

"What do you mean no?" I said placing my hands on the table. "We can't stay here, we have no future here. You know this. You have to come with me."

I was trying to stop the hurt of her rejection, but a knife-edged darkness cut deep. I was beginning to be consumed by the grind of my fears.

"No, I don't have to do that. I won't leave my family. Do you think your country is better than mine?"

"Not better, just a little freer." I felt tears and anger struggle for first place.

"No, Lu, I will not go." She folded her arms across her chest.

"Time after time you told me to trust your heart for me. Finally, I did and I do, and now I ask you to come with me for a life together, and you're saying no?" I was up, walking around the room, my strides lengthening. I stopped, put my hands on my hips. "Maybe you don't really love me after all."

Her eyes hardened. She was angry. "Stop telling me I don't love you. I am tired of these words. Always you don't believe me." She took the apple peel and began ripping it in chunks. "I found many ways to show you my deepest heart, you know this." Now pointing at me with a fragment of a ripped red peel, she continued. "Never tell me I don't love you." Her eyes flashed fury.

I was angry too. How could she say no? There was no future for us here. She must certainly know that too.

"Never mind then, I won't ask you again." I was still walking around the room, becoming more upset. "I'm going to leave now. I'm going to walk home."

"Fine. You go."

I grabbed my coat and satchel and went out the door. I took the steps down, two at a time. Reaching the outside, I leaned against the building. I was staggered by her rejection, angry and heart-broken. How could I have made such a mess of asking her to come with me? The frenzied, liquid emotion running through me hardened. Well then, the hell with it, and her. Maybe we just weren't meant to be together. I started walking the three miles back and decided to call Elizabeth when I got home.

Just as I turned onto the last road home, she rode by me. When she was sure I would see her, she put her nose up and put on extra speed.

When I got home, I found a note she had slipped under my door: *I am going to my village for three days.* After I spoke with Elizabeth, I put a note under her door: *I'm going to Hong Kong with Elizabeth. I don't know when I'll be back.*

FRAGRANT HARBOR

香港

"My god, Elizabeth, this suite is so swanky. I've never been in such a place."

"Pretty spiffy eh, Lu?"

"Yeah, I think so. It's so much fun to be in a really ritzy hotel."

She tipped the bellhop and I looked into the bathroom.

"Elizabeth, this bathroom is bigger than my room in Beijing. Is that a bidet? How do you use it?"

"I'll tell ya later mate, it's easy," she said leaning against the door, watching me explore our room, and laughing as I landed on one of the queen beds.

"Let's open the curtains," I said. I found a big green button, and when I pushed it, the floor to ceiling wrap-around drapes slowly opened to a sunset view of Victoria Harbor. We stood there, me with my mouth open, watching traditional junks, ferries, cruise ships and even oil tankers navigate the waters.

"Lu, slide a couple of chairs over here to the windows. Let's sit in comfort for a bit. And let's have a cocktail."

I opened the minibar and stood there, frozen by the

modernity. Had I forgotten the simple convenience of refrigeration so quickly?

"Lu, get your nose out of the fridge, will you? And sit down."

Handing her a small bottle of Glenlivet and a glass, I sat down and poured mine over ice.

"A toast to you, dear friend, for giving me this gift. It's really generous of you to pay for all of this."

"Lu, you are most welcome. We both needed to get out of town, especially you. You are a dear mate, ya know. Glad I could do it."

"Is this level of living, I mean this elegance, just normal for you?" I asked.

"Yeah," she answered quietly.

"Do you miss your ranch?"

"I miss riding my horses, driving a car, having proper furniture, good food, and my family and mates."

"I bet the difference between your ranch and China is huge," I said taking a sip of my drink. "For me, the real difference is the hardness of life. I am kind of poor, so the difference between my American stuff and China, like cars and furniture, isn't as great as yours."

"Don't let my wealth come between us, Lu," she said looking at me.

"Well, there is a difference. Maybe you'll want to do things I could never afford, or want me to return this gift in kind."

"No, I don't want anything back. I admire you, I like laughing with you, and want to be your friend."

We both fell silent. I wondered if she really meant it, paying my way and not expecting anything in return.

"My mom was without means when she married my dad, so she knows both sides. She taught my sisters and me that money can come and go, but true friends last forever."

"I want to take care of the tips then, just so I feel more comfortable. Okay?"

"You got it, mate."

We were quiet, watching the vessels track around the harbor and the city lights brightening as the sun went down. I missed Ming terribly. I wanted her to see this with me. I had to blink back a few tears to clear my vision.

If Elizabeth noticed, she gave no clue and got two more bottles of Glenlivet and more ice for me. While she poured, we decided that tomorrow, after she went to the bank, we would window shop and maybe even buy the gifts she wanted to bring back to Beijing.

Elizabeth stood up and stretched. Then walked over to the desk, picked up two room service menus, and handed one to me. "Lu," she said, "order anything you want."

I ran my finger down the page: salads, steak, baked potatoes, peach pie, and so much more. I had to put the menu down for a minute.

"It's all a bit much, isn't it?"

"Yeah. I think maybe I've been in China too long," I said. "After nearly a year and a half of living a third-world life, I have to reacquaint myself with my old normal."

After studying the menu for a few more minutes, I had my order. "I'd like a steak, baked potato with lots of butter and extra sour cream, and a green salad with Roquefort dressing."

"Me too. I'll call it in."

While on hold, she spoke again. "Hey, Lu, we can order an in-house movie after we eat, if you want."

I picked up a card listing the viewing options. "Hmm, says here that we can choose *Return of the Jedi* or *Octopussy*."

We both looked at each other and laughed.

Room service placed our dinners on the table, and after I tipped the waiter, we sat down and looked at the food, then at each other and began to laugh. We were like giddy little girls getting to eat the whole cake at a birthday party.

After we finished eating I placed the dishes on the cart and rolled it outside the door.

"Show me how to use the bidet?" I asked as I closed the room door.

"Okay, so you turn on the water, but put your hand over the bubbler so it doesn't shoot all over the room. Check that the temp isn't too hot, and sit down. After you do your business, use these towels."

"I want to try it now, then I'm gonna take a shower."

"Go for it."

"Elizabeth, these towels are heated and these bathrobes too," I yelled. I heard her laugh.

The shower was spacious with dark brown tiles and a gold-color grout. The floor was slightly roughed slate and there were jets and sprays from dozens of different places. I was enjoying the luxury of it all—and then I missed Ming. Again. I wanted her with me. I put my arms on the wall and sobbed. Maybe I shouldn't have pushed her to decide, maybe I shouldn't have even asked. I just didn't want to lose her. And still, a stubborn tiny hope refused to die; maybe she would change her mind. Then I cursed myself; I was being a goddamn fool.

When Elizabeth finished her shower, she turned on the television, handed me one of two big bowls of popcorn she had ordered, and we watched *Octopussy*. We hooted and catcalled and laughed, and when it ended, we turned off the lights.

"I heard you crying in the shower. Are you all right, mate?"

"No, I'm really not."

"I know. It hurts like hell."

"I'm so angry at her for not wanting to come with me. Why can't she see that this is the right way for us? Is there something I missed, something I didn't understand?"

She came and sat next to me, comforting me.

"This isn't how it was supposed to be, is it, mate?" She got a towel and handed it to me and I blew my nose. "It's sure as hell not what you dreamed of, is it?" she asked.

"I feel so deeply alone Elizabeth, and yes, it hurts like hell." I turned onto my stomach. She stroked my back with her hand, soothing me. "I just don't know what to do."

"I feel so bad, it hurts me to see you suffer. Let's figure out a plan while we're here. Maybe there's something I can do to help."

In the morning we walked two short blocks to the Star Ferry. We rode across the bay to the Kowloon side, sitting on the top deck in front. I pushed my face into the mist and the wind that the boat carved around us.

Kowloon was just waking up. The neon signs were a pageant of Chinese characters, dancing in a haze of fog. As we walked south, the people around us spoke in tumbles of British English and Cantonese. Street vendors began lighting their burners, and the smell of cooking oil reaching temperature and propane gas stirred the air. A Rolls Royce glided beside chugging taxis. The shopkeepers began rolling up aluminum doors displaying electronics from the cheapest to the best.

"This way Lu. We're going to eat the best congee, pickles and ghosts you'll ever have."

We stepped around three young girls filling every last inch of their grill with marinated kabobs and I crashed right into an old Hakka woman. The collision knocked off her bamboo hat with curtain-like fringe and sent her basket of oranges sprawling onto the wet sidewalk. Horrified, I scrambled to help, but she was annoyed with me and batted me away. I retrieved her hat, and as I handed it to her, she started to scream at me in Cantonese.

"Lu, c'mon." Elizabeth grabbed my hand and hurried me away. "She needs to save face."

Several blocks later, we entered a restaurant with five two-person tables. I sat down at the only vacant one as Elizabeth ordered at the counter, then sat down across from me.

"I feel awful about that woman," I said.

"I know, but forget about it. She'll have a good story to tell at home tonight."

The woman behind the counter soon gestured for Elizabeth to get the food.

"This is terrific congee," I said. "The pickles are really good and the ghosts are just right. How much is my share?"

"About twenty cents," she laughed.

"I want to go to a lesbian bar tonight and dance," I said. "Do you know any?"

"No, there aren't any, just dyke bars."

"Hey, call your hamburger friend."

"Can't, she's in France, noodling with a gorgeous Argentinian tennis player."

"So, now what?"

"Here's what we do. We get a taxi and ask him to take us to a men's bar. We tell him we're looking for your brother and you need to save him. Got it?"

"Yep."

"Then when we get to the boys' bar, we ask where the girls are."

"Brilliant."

We ate our fill and walked to the Financial District, where Elizabeth had some ranch business to take care of at the Hong Kong and Shanghai Bank. She handed the manager her card and we sat down in soft leather chairs that must have been there for a hundred years. A few minutes later, a higher-level manager came and invited her to an upstairs office.

I remained in the comfortable chair, watching the bustle on the street. It was then that a tiny thought of leaving the Institute and returning to the States began to take shape. I started to consider what to pack up and how to get my exit visa. I couldn't stay there and see Ming every day, knowing we had no future. It would be hard on her too, so the best plan was to leave.

"I want to go to the Hong Kong Mall," Elizabeth said, tapping me on my shoulder. "There's a store there I want to visit.

Do you mind?"

"Sounds good. What kind of store?"

"I'll tell ya on the way. Let's go."

I stared out the taxi window, watching the city whiz by. The Hong Kongers were fast-busy. There were rich people and not so rich, Bentleys and burdened tricycles, well-crafted gabardine suits and dingy tee shirts and stained shorts. Everyone was out to make a buck or make it big, and there was no time to lose. I could feel the energy through the taxi window.

"I want to get some sexy lingerie for Guan."

She saw me wince and asked what was wrong. I told her I was beginning to think about leaving Beijing as soon as possible, and she grabbed my arm.

"You can't leave. I know it will hurt to see Ming, but just avoid her. Finish your studies then go and get that UN job."

"I just couldn't avoid her, I know me. Really, it's best I leave."

"Aw Christ mate. Listen goddammit, you are not leaving. We're going to think of a plan and then we'll make it work."

Elizabeth paid the taxi fare and we entered a sculpted-marble shopping mall. Everything was shiny, upscale. The floors were marble and all of the shops' glass windows were framed in bronze.

The lighting in the lingerie store was subdued; there was a vanilla scent in the air. In the panty section a salesgirl asked if she could help. Elizabeth shook her head.

"You wanna get a pair for Ming? She might love ya for 'em—"

"No, I want to get a Teflon frying pan."

"Lu," she said leaning her arm on the counter. "That's so damn romantic. You really know how to win a girl's heart." She looked down and shook her head. "A frying pan."

I was a little defensive. "When I am gone, she can remember me as practical. And besides, it will help with the cooking oil rationing."

114

"Sheesh, get her the panties too, dammit. You can seduce her with them. Then she will go with you anywhere."

I gave in. Something in Elizabeth's suggestion was appealing. Maybe she had touched my tiny hope.

"Elizabeth, I don't know her size in British sizing," I whispered.

"You know her butt, figure it out."

"Turn around then, and let me measure them against you. Hmmm, she has more muscle than you, but let me see how these might work."

I held several different sizes against her, imagining Ming's fit.

"Lu, you're getting me hot."

"Is it the red ones or the black pair that are stirring you up?"

Elizabeth laughed.

I chose a pair in red and Elizabeth chose two in red and two in pink. We both opted for the free gift-wrapping, a sophisticated layering of soft browns and a dark brown velvet bow. We each paid and Elizabeth arranged to have them sent to the hotel. I wondered what I was doing, how Ming would receive this gift from the decadent West. Would she even want a gift from me?

"I'm hungry," I said.

"I know a place," she said. "Would you like some dim sum?"

"Are you serious? Absolutely."

"The restaurant is just up the street. Let's go."

She took my elbow and we started walking. "How about some crispy chicken feet?"

"I don't know about that, you know. I mean, they are really icky."

"Nah, nah, they're tasty."

"I remember. You served them to me when I came to your place the first time and I didn't like them," I said as we stepped out of the way of four boys on skateboards.

"It's hard to get in, it's very popular," she said yelling over the racket of the metal wheels.

I stopped us in the middle of the sidewalk. "So you're saying we'll wait in line for a while?"

"Maybe a little, mate. I'll see if I can grease our way to the head of the line."

We walked about a half a block more and she said the entrance to the restaurant was just on the left, which was obvious by the long line of people waiting to get in.

"Elizabeth, that line is ungodly long. Let's eat somewhere else."

"Yeah. Let's go back to the hotel then."

In the taxi she chatted with the driver. I rolled down the window, wanting the street noise to wash over me, distract me from thoughts of Ming.

When we got to the suite, I saw that our purchases were on the table. Elizabeth noticed that she only had two pillows instead of her requested four. She bee-lined for the telephone.

Several short minutes later there was a knock on the door. I answered it and in came a uniformed man carrying an extra-large fruit basket. Behind him was a distraught-looking housekeeper bearing two pillows.

I noticed that his name badge indicated he was a supervisor and he wordlessly berated the woman. He was very apologetic to Elizabeth, as was the housekeeper as she placed and plumped the pillows on Elizabeth's bed.

He, with restraint, ushered the woman out of the room as I held the door open for them. Once in the hallway, he started throwing things from her housekeeping cart onto the floor and yelling at her to clean up the mess. She was clearly upset and yet he continued to throw things from her cart.

I slammed the door closed so he would know his behavior had been witnessed.

I leaned against the closed door, stunned by what I had seen. I looked at Elizabeth, framed with the light from the wide windows.

She turned toward me, surprised by the loud bang of the door. "What was that?"

I walked toward the windows, pulled two chairs over and we sat down.

I told her about the events and slumped in my chair.

"Motherfucker," she cursed. "I'll call room service and order for us. Maybe I'll even ask to speak to the chief executive while I'm at it. Bastard."

While she phoned room service, I sat thinking of the juxtaposition of plenty and minimal, that some could pay thousands to eat exotic dishes and others could afford only a bowl of rice. Some had privileges and permissions, and many didn't. I had been selfish when I asked Ming to come to the States. I hadn't fully considered what she might want or would have to give up. I had been thoughtless of her needs.

Before Elizabeth returned to her chair, I decided to have one final conversation with Ming. And Elizabeth and I would buy a frying pan tomorrow.

WHISPERING

耳语

I had been gone for nearly six days, the three I stayed with Elizabeth while I secured my travel permissions and visas, and our two days in Hong Kong, plus travel.

Sitting back at the desk in my room in the late afternoon, tracing a crack in the cement floor with my eyes, I felt a familiar stretch. I was straddling a first world and a third world. Again.

I'd unpacked and put away everything except for the frying pan and the gift box. I felt Ming's absence deep in my bones. I wanted to go to her, to hold her and talk with her. I wanted her skin, her mouth; I wanted to press her into the deepest part of my soul and never let her go.

I slipped my gifts into a pillowcase, wondering when I would give them to her, and if they would be our goodbye. I put them into my wardrobe without an answer and sat down again at my desk, then opened my grammar book, wondering how far I might be behind. Then I thought, maybe it didn't matter since I would be leaving in a matter of weeks.

I was about to make some coffee when I heard a light tapping on my door. There she was. We stood just looking at each other for a moment, and then she came in and closed the door.

We stood awkwardly, not knowing what to do, what to say. This was the first time we had seen each other in a week. We stood apart and fidgeted, then ran and crashed into each other, crying. Our tears made our faces and lips slick. We began removing each other's clothes and fell onto my bed. I felt her wet on my thigh and slid my fingers fully between her legs, took her left nipple into my mouth. She arched her back, and her breath caught. She moaned deeply, and I held her as she came, just as she liked. I listened to her catching her breath in my ear.

She rolled me onto my back. We were glow-slippery. She slid and kissed herself down my body leaving a trail of juice and opened my legs with hers. Her touch was firm and swift. I was wild, shuddering and growling. And then I disconnected. I had switched my body off.

"Lu?"

Not sure myself, I gave her a facile answer. "I don't know, tired from travel probably."

I was surprised I had lost that orgasm with her. It had never happened before. But I had pulled back. I needed to protect myself.

She wound herself tight to me, pressing together our pubic bones. I felt her wetness flowing into mine. I took in her sweet scent, felt her braid on my shoulder. Holding her body, feeling her weight, stroking her back, I allowed myself to savor her.

"Lu, I came every day to see if you were back. I came to your door many times each day. I worried you might never come back."

"I'm glad to hear you missed me. I wasn't sure." I hugged her a little closer.

She found her comfort, and continued. "Lu, when I was home I talked with Ma about leaving and she forbade me. First she said America is full of robbers. On the second day she told me there were too many bad ghosts, ghosts who eat babies and kill people like me."

"What did you say?" My stomach clenched and I stopped caressing the back of her neck with my thumb.

"Nothing. She doesn't really believe in ghosts. She wanted to scare me."

She adjusted herself onto my right side and continued. "On my last day she told me if I left, she would never forgive me."

I closed my eyes and felt my tiny hope dim; it seemed that our end was close. If her mother wouldn't forgive her, then I was sure there was no chance that she would come with me.

"What were you thinking about all those days?" I asked.

"At first I couldn't think. Both choices were too big. Late on the second day I went to feed the pigs. They were happy. Every day the same: eat, wiggle, sleep, and make noises. They have a good life, just like me." She sighed and rolled up onto her elbow. Looking at me she said, "I want to be even happier than the pigs."

I didn't speak. I knew she wasn't finished. I waited for her. I reached out and touched her face with my fingertips.

"We must be together. I want your heart forever," she said. "I want you to stay here and be with me. I also want to go to your country."

Her tears started to roll down her cheeks and onto my fingers. "I still don't know to choose." She trembled a little. Still I waited.

"But maybe you don't want me anymore, Lu. Maybe I lost your heart when you stayed in Hong Kong."

I wiped a few tears from her cheek. "When I was in Hong Kong I decided to return to America as soon as I could. I knew I couldn't stay here and not have a future with you. And I thought you might want me to leave too." I took her hand. "I have never loved anyone as much as you and I would give you everything I have to keep that. But, Ming, I'm not sure. I mean, now I wonder if it would be such a good idea to have you leave everything you know and love to come with me."

Her body slumped a little on her elbow and her head dropped slightly. "You asked me to go, so this is for me to say, not you." She looked me square in the eye. "I know you, I need to tell you every way that I love you until you believe me again." She slid her hand into my hair and said, "We hurt each other and I am sorry for my part."

"I'm sorry for hurting you too, I really am. I was thoughtless."

She laid herself fully on me and we wrapped ourselves together. "Let's just see how things go before we make decisions," I said.

We held each other, with an edge of unease, for a fast hour. The sun began to go down and the light softened around us.

"I have some small cream cakes I bought at the airport. Let's eat them and I'll make you some tea."

After I plugged in the hot plate and she put water into the pot, we sat on the edge of the bed and began to dress. I stood before her and held her face up. Then I knelt down in front of her and kissed her deep. I wanted to find her heart, to know if I could still trust her. She kissed me back and it was there, everything I needed to know.

"Do you want tea or coffee, Lu?"

"I want some coffee," I said setting the little cakes on a plate.

"I'll make it. You teach me."

I handed her two squares of toilet paper and showed her how to fold and tuck them into the thermos cap. She had never asked to learn this before. Could I take this gesture as a delicate indication? I smiled at her while she spooned the coffee into the cap and I showed her how to bloom the coffee.

Handing me a cup, she asked, "Good, Lu?"

"Best ever."

She smiled at me with a proud, tiny wink.

I sat her tea, my coffee, and the cake plate on the desk and sat across from her.

"When I asked you to come with me," I said, wrapping my fingers around my cup, "I didn't fully consider what I was asking of you and what it might mean to you, what you might have to give up. When I was in Hong Kong I began to understand this."

She took my fingers from my cup, knitted them with hers, and remained silent.

"We both have a lot on the line with this decision," I said looking at our hands. "If you leave, Ma may never forgive you. If you come with me, I will be responsible for us for quite a while. It'll just be me to earn money until you find a job. We'll have to find a cheap place to live and we'll need to buy food, maybe a car and pay bills. There's a lot to think about."

This time she was quiet; she waited for me.

"Life in the States will be more complicated and faster than here. We might be a little freer than here, but not by much. But if we are together, I think we can make a great life."

She let go of my hand and got up to put her cup in the dishpan. Turning toward me, she said, "I want you stay the night with me, but I want to think about my choice. Will you come to me in an hour?"

"Of course," I said standing up next to her, gently pulling her to me. We just held each other for a few moments and then she left.

She was right, the decision was hers to make. If she wasn't going to come with me, then I would definitely leave. I couldn't let myself love her more each day and then have to separate. I also came to understand that I needed to be exceptionally clear that Julia's palimpsest of broken promises could be truly overwritten by Ming's abiding love for me, and mine for her.

When I turned on my desk lamp, I realized that nearly two hours had passed.

She was in bed when I opened her door. I blew out the candle she had left lit for me, took off my clothes and slid in next to her. I really wanted to ask her if she had made a decision, but

I knew to wait for her to tell me.

As we settled in and kissed good night, she said, "Lu, there is no school tomorrow. I want go to the Temple of Heaven and get the pot for the flower. Will you come with me?"

"Sure, let's go first thing."

In the morning, hand in hand, we walked silently to the bus stop. We were connected and pensive. I was weighing the possibilities of where our futures might lie, wondering if we even had a future. I had questioned the depth of my proposal to her for many days, weeks really. I now knew I could give her my complete commitment; the rest was up to her.

The bus arrived and she bought the tickets. I squirmed down the aisle behind her, crunching sunflower seed shells that littered the evenly spaced joists that formed the floor. We wiggled through workers, shoppers, and old men with songbirds in bamboo cages, finally finding space in the back of the bus. When I held onto the head-high steel bar and looked down to her face, there was that golden glow I had come to love so deeply. She leaned discreetly, just so, into me. I held my ground firm against her. We kept this balance, adjusting to the pitch and roll of the rickety Russian-made bus.

We changed buses at Ping An Li and I lost her in the masses of people pushing to get off the bus and the folks straining to board. Everywhere I looked it was the same: padded coats and black hair.

I stayed where I was, knowing it was easier for her to find me since I was the single blond-haired person in that chaos of black. I scanned for her, feeling increasingly alone. Just before despair began to root, she returned and saw the ache in my searching eyes.

Putting her hand on her hip, she said in English:

"Lu, you are silly. I am here. I got Elephant Ears for us. Now we eat."

The pastries were shaped like a very small elephant's ear, flat,

123

fried crispy, and dripping with honey.

We found a small space on a crowded bench, sat down and wrested a bit more room with our hips. I held her in the corner of my eye. I would miss these tiny moments, the street food, peanuts, bicycle rides, and everything *her*. I was beginning to store up these minutes with her to remember when I was gone.

She leaned a little closer to me, and whispered in English, "I feel you holding me with your eye. I love you, Lu, from my deepest and extra heart. This will always be true."

"No matter where we are?" I asked in a small seizing voice.

"Yes."

We were both silent for a long moment. She swallowed her bite of pastry, and then spoke.

"I want to be quiet now, I want to think."

I walked a half step behind her to the next bus stop, almost thinking, mostly opaque.

"Quiet your heart," she said softly in Chinese as we queued at the bus stop.

The #11 bus belched into the terminus. This time I bought the tickets. Noticing that I was a foreigner speaking their language, some passengers wanted conversation with me. I had no interest in answering their questions; I wanted my place, tight, in close with her. I was polite, however, and chatted with them in Chinese for a few minutes, then I respectfully wished them full bellies.

I struggled through the people, the poultry, finches, and garlic breath to her side. As the bus pulled from the stop, the gears were ground by the unskilled driver and we lurched forward. I grabbed the steel bar just in time to catch her and steady several riders around me. After we settled ourselves, she translated a comment from a passenger nearby.

"She said the bus driver is too stupid to do this job. He should go back to the countryside and plow fields with the wind from his ass."

"Can farts be that powerful?"

"If you're really stupid, yes."

I turned my gaze from her and stared out the window, watching the fluidity of the people; their rhythms hummed ancient. Their strains and struggles, grunts and hopes also lived in Ming's blood, the blood of dragons, and propelled her without her intention.

Finally, I caught sight of the Temple of Heaven, our destination. It was first constructed in 1420, in the eighteenth year of the reign of the Ming emperor, the place where the emperors worshiped the god of heaven and prayed for a good harvest. I imagined the road being scuffed by the millions of people who had trod thousands of miles to live their simple lives. Here we were, two very different women leaving this people's bus, deeply joined and stepping onto land of profound and exacting ritual.

"Where are the pots and the marketplace? Didn't we come here to get a pot for your hyacinth bulb?"

"The pots are on the outside of the wall, to the west. We will go there next," she said.

Round altar buildings, supported on thick redwood pillars, blazed celestial blue, imperial red and yellow, their brilliance nearly blinding in the cloudless sky. We walked along a tree-lined path to a wall of grey-brown bricks, about 600 yards long and 12 feet high. She stopped walking and told me to stand three feet from her.

"You are farther from me," she said. "Do you still know I love you?"

"Yes," I answered, curious, uneasy about what she might have in mind.

"Now go halfway to that bridge," she pointed. "Then go to the wall, face to the north and put your ear on the wall."

I walked to the midway point; my gut clutched with each step from her. I was nearly convinced she would vanish. I turned slightly to make sure she was still there; she was. Reaching halfway, I stopped and looked back. She touched her ear and pointed to the wall. I turned from her, facing north, and put my ear to the wall.

"Can you hear me tell you I love you?" I heard her whisper.

Astonished, I whispered back, "Yes."

"Go now to the end of the wall and listen for me again," she whispered.

Reaching the end, with my back still to her, I again put my ear to the wall.

"Do you still love me, Lu?"

"Yes," I said. "I do."

"I will go with you to America," she whispered last.

I turned toward her and watched her approach. Her steps quickened, and when she was next to me, she took my hand.

Holding her hand tightly, I asked, "Are you sure, really sure? What about Ma?"

"I am sure now, Lu." In Chinese she said, "*Yong yuen.* Forever."

We started walking to the west, toward the promised shopping area. Her face carried the same supreme joy that I felt in my heart. She stopped for a second; her eyes twinkled.

"Lu, when we get home, I hope you won't be tired."

I threw my head back and laughed out loud. She did too.

Walking through a fragrant rose garden, nearing the west gate, I asked her, "What was that magical wall called?"

"The Whispering Wall. The men who protected the emperor whispered his condition all night for his safety."

We passed though the west gate and slammed into a boisterous, celebrating marketplace. Multicolored paper lanterns, dragons and cartoon characters hung from every available spot. There were scores of songbirds and double that of bamboo cages. Sweet potatoes and peanuts were roasting, wafting intoxicating smoke and aroma into the air.

I started to walk toward a growing crowd of people as several soldiers pasted official notices on a wall. The posters had large red characters and I was curious.

"Not now," she said. "We can read them later."

She took my sleeve and aimed us to the pot sellers. Several potters had good skill, their glazes artfully applied.

"The flower is purple," she reminded. "The color must be right."

We moved along the tables, considering several, rejecting others. I saw one just ahead and reached for it.

"This one, I like the mauve color, it reminds me of a sunrise," I said.

"I want this one. You are right, it is very good."

"I will do the talking," she giggled. "I will tell him I am your cook, then he will give us a good price."

I was laughing too and had to turn away for a moment, gathering myself. Then I stood behind her and scowled like an entitled employer. She bargained with the craggy-faced potter for my generous foreigner's discount and bought the pot with the money I had given her before we left home.

She took the pot from the merchant, who had deftly crafted a protective wrapper and string handles and cradled it in her arms.

"Let's go home, I want to do nice things with you."

We walked side by side, quietly graced by our fine new promise. The final merchants, birds, and raucous bustle of the marketplace quieted behind us. We stood near a tree and held hands while waiting for the bus.

"Tomorrow I'll call the embassy and ask Alice about visas," I said, squeezing her hand. "And, I have gifts for you from Hong Kong."

She looked down, circling the dirt with the toe of her right shoe for a moment. Then looked up at me with her sweet smile and said, "I want your gifts."

The #11 bus arrived and I bought the tickets while she found a place for us in the back. I slid through the ubiquitous workers, shoppers, poultry, and vegetables to stand with her.

She held her pot in her arms and leaned softly, discreetly into me.

When I reached up to hold the overhead bar, through the bus window I saw more soldiers putting up posters on another wall.

SPIRITUAL POLLUTION

精 神 污 染

Ming whisked through my door, came up behind me, and hugged me.

"Come to my room now." Her whispers tickled my ear. "I need your help."

"What's up?"

"Cooking."

"I'll be right down," I said as she hustled out the door.

I grabbed the pillowcase and then hid it behind my back as I entered her room.

"Close your eyes, I brought you the gifts."

I handed her the pillowcase. She pulled the frying pan out first. She looked at the cooking surface, questioning with her eyes. "It's a new technology," I explained. "Things won't stick, so you won't need as much oil to cook." Running her fingers over the surface, she began to understand, her face breaking into a smile. Then she hugged it to her chest and thanked me.

I was encouraged that I might be doing well in the gift department and held my breath as she pulled out the classy brown box.

She just held it, shifting it from one hand to another, as though it had an internal heat source. Then, without opening it, without explanation, she put it in her wardrobe and closed the door. I looked to her face for a clue as to why she didn't open it; there was none. She acted as if everything was normal. And, as I would learn, it was.

"I am making a dinner for you, we must finish the cooking. Sit there on your stool."

We were silent, sitting side by side on the short stools, watching the little dough pillows rising and sinking in the gentle boil. She guided them carefully with a wire ladle gripped with a split bamboo handle that her mother had fashioned for her. She stood up and turned away from me, putting vinegar and soy sauce into two white bowls. I looked at her, framed in this simple room, saw the simple life we shared, where everything was just enough, nothing was extra, and nothing essential was missing. I felt a little heart sting knowing I would miss this life we had made. I knew she would too, more than either of us could probably know right now. I hoped I would be up for the tasks of our relocation and not let her down.

"Hold this plate," she said lifting out all the *jiao zi*. She then slid four in each bowl and handed me one and a pair of chopsticks and sat down next to me.

They were perfect. The balance of pork, vegetables, and sesame oil was sublime. I closed my eyes and savored their exquisite flavor.

"Lu," she said leaning on my knee. "I want to learn to drive a car in America. Will you teach me this?"

"You bet."

"I also want to choose my own job," she said in a lower voice. "I don't want old men deciding what I should do for the rest of my life. Maybe I might want two jobs."

"You can do this, no doubt," I said. "Anything else?"

"I want to meet your friends, go to the Grand Canyon, eat

130

pizza, learn to dance, have a big bed—and why are you laughing?"

"Your wishes," I giggled, "are delightful and all over the place. I'll teach you to drive and dance anytime you want. We'll buy a big bed first thing. And find a glorious job for you too."

She looked down to the pot, gently scooping up the last bits of jiao zi. "Lu, I will be leaving with you and I want to give the new pan to Ma, do you mind?"

"I think that's a good idea. Have you told her yet?"

"I called to her this morning. She said she knew I would choose you."

"Was she angry?"

"Maybe. She cried a little and asked me to come home very soon. I will miss her, Lu."

I put my arm around her shoulder and hugged her. "I know you will, I'll miss her for you too. We'll do everything we can to come and visit someday."

I rose to offer more dumplings; she declined. She stood up next to me putting the dishes into the big pan.

"Sweetcakes, those were the best ever."

"Lu," she said bumping her hip into mine. "You say that every time."

"And I mean it every time. C'mon, let's go do the dishes."

We stood together in the laundry room waiting for the seven o'clock hot water's arrival; the spigot was turned on and one of us would occasionally wave a finger under the still-cold stream.

"Ming, this morning I was walking down the stairs behind my teacher and he said to his friend that he was going to hide his Mozart sheet music."

Her expression clouded for an instant. "What did his friend say?"

"I'm not sure, I couldn't hear everything. I think he said it would be a good idea. Why would he want to hide his music?"

"I don't know," she replied with a little irritation in her voice. "Come to me after your homework, I want you to stay the night with me."

We didn't talk about the possibilities swirling around us, even though they were present between us. In the morning we shared a *mantou*, like a large steamed biscuit, and cups of warm water and left for school.

When Ming turned her bike to the left, I caught up with Helen, my New Zealand classmate, and we began quizzing each other on the idioms we had had to learn overnight.

"Louise, what does this mean? 牢不可破. *lao bu ke po.*"

"Unbreakable, like a stout heart or a good friendship."

"Good on ya. Now ask me one."

"Okay, here's yours, 生龙活虎. *sheng long huo hu.*"

She thought for a few seconds as we rolled through the display of calligraphy. "Brave as a dragon, lively as a tiger, full of vim and vigor."

"You got it. Jeez, I hope we don't have a test before Friday."

"Naw, we won't. Hey, what's happened to all the boys' hair?" Helen pointed. "Yesterday they all had curly hair."

"By god you're right. I wonder why?"

We continued along the short green hedges nearing the classroom building when I noticed that our teachers' clothing had changed too.

"Louise, our teachers are wearing their old padded coats again."

"Helen, this is making me nervous."

"Bloody hell. Don't look anymore, let's just go to class."

At the morning break, the hallways were filled with nervous chatter. I overheard some Swedish students say that several of their Chinese friends were missing. My heart squinched at the thought that Ming might be caught up in this.

I ran up the stairs two at a time to her office, and opened the door to a bright, sunlit room. Her second-rate hot plate was waging a losing battle to warm the air around her. She was seated at her desk, wearing gloves and her big blue coat that I hadn't seen since last year. She was reading *The People's Daily*, 人民日报.

"What's going on?" I asked, sliding into the chair next to her desk. "My classmates are tense and edgy. We see that people's clothing and hairstyles have changed overnight."

Without taking her eyes off the paper, she answered, "I'm not sure."

Picking up a pencil, I drummed on her desk.

"Well, what's in the newspaper? Any news, any clues?"

I noticed that the date under the flag was two days earlier, so there might not be any mention. The paper was the mouthpiece of the Communist Party, so it was also likely that whatever was written would be truncated and self-serving.

"Go back to class," she said in a soft, measured tone. Scrunching the paper inward and looking at me around the folds, she said, "After class, go to your dining hall, get your lunch, then come to my room and we will talk."

Returning to class, it was becoming clear that whatever was going on was problematic, immediate, and begat whispers of alarm. Too much had changed so quickly. My teachers were nervous, frequently glancing at the door, and that made us jittery. Without accurate information we became even more susceptible to the faintest wisp of rumor floating by. Most frequently murmured was that all intellectuals would be again sent to the countryside for reeducation. That would mean Ming, Guan, my teachers, and others.

When I walked into her room, Ming was standing, looking out of her window. I set my lunch on her desk and walked up behind her and put my arms around her and kissed her neck.

"Do you know what is going on yet?"

"No," she said leaning back into me. "I have pieces, but I still don't know."

"How can we find out?"

Turning around and laying her head on my chest, she said,

133

"I am not sure yet."

"Are you scared?" I asked, hugging her a little closer.

"Yes, a little bit."

"I am scared quite a bit," I said. "I am afraid we might float away on a tide of political upheaval."

"Right now we can't know," she said kissing me then unwinding our hug. Getting two plates, she said, "Maybe we shouldn't think this."

"Okay then, let's eat," I said. I had an inkling that she wasn't telling me everything she knew. Her posture suggested held burdens.

I halved the noodles, the *dou fu*, and white cabbage. She put her potatoes and pork slivers on each of our plates, and then poured hot water into cups over jasmine tea.

"Sleep with me for our nap. Then I must take our school bus to another work unit for a teachers' meeting. I will be back after seven."

"Shall I make dinner?"

"No, I will eat with them. I will come to you when I return."

When she left to wash the dishes, I peeked into her wardrobe to see if she had opened the gift. It was still sitting just where she had put it the night before.

We dried the dishes, took off our blouses and bras and settled on her bed for a nap that the whole of China took at midday. Finding our fit, we slept lightly.

I decided I wanted to find Wang, my young friend from the post office, instead of doing my homework. Ming didn't like him; she thought he was wild and untethered, that he had ideas against the government that could bring trouble.

I rode my bike to Wu Dao Kou hoping to find him. Something mysterious was going on, and there might be danger. Wang might know. He, like most Chinese, had the advantage of *xiao dao xiao xi*, "little road news," which was a more verifiable form of gossip.

I was glad it was cold; being bundled up in my fur hat and cotton facemask helped prevent announcing myself as a foreigner. I was nervous. I noticed there were menacing official posters on the walls like the ones Ming and I had seen at the Temple of Heaven. I studied them. My eyes widened when I recognized their consequence. There were names of people, in red. They were publications of death warrants. I winced when I remembered being told that the families of those executed were sent the bill for the bullet to the head. Three cents.

I found Wang in front of the post office, making his stamp deals. His hair was freshly shorn, like all the other young men, revealing a ragged tan line. He caught my eye and hooked his thumb for me to meet him behind the butcher shop. We walked quickly, separately, to the bicycle racks.

Unlocking our bikes, he said without looking at me, "Wang Fu Jing."

Wang Fu Jing is a shopping area often frequented by tourists. It would be safer to talk there. I rode my bike with my eyes forward. Suddenly, silently he was by my side.

"Wang," I asked, "what is happening to the people?"

"I only know this," he began, mostly in Chinese with a sprinkle of English. "This trouble is called 'Spiritual Pollution.' Deng Xiao Ping started this. We are afraid we will have another Cultural Revolution. All the men cut their hair so they don't look Western. We really don't know what to do. Now we will all be very careful again and stay small."

His face creased with worry; I had never seen him without his confident swagger. He told me that his older brother had been arrested and sentenced to thirty days in a Beijing jail for watching a pirated videotape of *Dallas* from Hong Kong.

"Wang, perhaps we should not be seen together. Is there danger here for me too?"

"You could be sent home if the Secret Police think you are a troublemaker. But you are a foreign student and you pay your own way, so the danger for you is small. Do not go to the Western Gate of Qing Hua University where I showed you to watch for the 'chicken girls' and the 'slit sleeves.' I think it won't be convenient for you to buy stamps for a while."

I remembered the day when he explained that 'chicken girls' was slang for prostitutes. Even richer was the use of 'slit sleeves.' The legend held that a scholar was in his garden writing poetry and his male lover fell asleep on his robe. Rather than disturb his sleep, he cut off the sleeve of his garment, and his lover remained undisturbed. So slang for gay men became 'slit sleeves.'

"What about you? What will you do, will you be safe, where will you go?"

"I will go to the countryside, deep beyond the Big Star People's Commune. You can look for me next Thursday at the post office at Wu Dao Kou. If I am not there, don't look for me, because you cannot get past the checkpoints."

"Xiao Wang, I—"

With a quick shake he slipped his graceful hand from mine and was gone. I swung my leg back over my bicycle. I could only look down. I breathed out an icy, visible breath, and pushed down hard on the pedals to return home.

About seven thirty Ming came to my room. "How was your meeting?" I asked, hugging her, holding her close.

"Quiet, people were careful with each other," she said hugging me back, pressing her pubic bone to mine, wiggling a little.

"Do you have questions about your homework?" she asked, smiling, pouring water for some tea and sitting down next to me.

"I didn't do my homework, I went to find Wang instead. He told me things you haven't."

"You must stay away from him, he is not good. I told you this."

"What does 'not good' mean?" I asked leaning on my elbows.

"He spends too much time at the post office selling stamps.

He has no job, and he talks with men who speak out about the government."

"Oh, I see," I said feeling defensive. "Well, you wouldn't tell me what's going on; I wanted to know, so I went to find him."

"You must do what I say in these matters," she said splaying her hands flat on my desk for emphasis. "You don't know about these things. You might make trouble and not even know it."

"I am scared for us," I fired back. "When I don't know things I get nervous; to calm myself I seek information."

"I am not telling you what I know because I am not sure what I know." She leaned forward and continued. "I am not keeping things from you. Rumors can cause damage."

"Well, sometimes I wonder why you won't just tell me before you know."

She told me what Wang had said. The movement was called Spiritual Pollution and no one knew just yet what it might mean. For Ming it meant more. Wang was too young to know the misery and terror of the Cultural Revolution. Ming's oldest sister had died of starvation and she had heard stories of her neighbors doing desperate things to avoid hunger and slow death. Ming had joined the Red Guards, not from conviction but from expediency, to remain a short nail.

I figured there might be more to know, about her past and Spiritual Pollution, but for now it could wait.

DETAINED

挽留了

Against Ming's advice, I did go to the Wu Dao Kou Post Office to search for Wang. She had warned me to stay away from him and post offices because in the innocuous barter of postage stamps there were conversations, talk that sometimes veered to sedition. But I wanted to know what was going on with the regular people, and if other dangers might be lying in wait.

I parked my bike and moved quietly, discreetly as I could for a tall blonde foreigner, among the stamp collectors and sellers. I asked for the first-day covers that I knew were widely available; I was only intent on overhearing conversations about the potential upheaval. I kept my eye on the periphery of the crowd, hoping Wang would arrive and I could catch his eye.

A man behind me asked, "Do you want to see these stamps?"

I turned to him, curious about what he might be offering. His eyes were not friendly, his smile a trick. Silently, two other men appeared, one on each side of me.

"Where do you live?" was his second question.

I foolishly lied, thinking he might not really know—a little test, and said: "Beijing University."

"No," he said leaning towards me, his face too close to mine, "you don't."

My knees wobbled. My mouth seemed to fill with dozens of dumplings that blocked speech and breath. The people nearby began to slowly drift away.

"You will come with us," he ordered.

Each of the men on either side of me took one of my arms. I tried to shake them off, but their grip was firm. I was escorted to a long black car not far from the post office. One man sat next to me in the back seat. The questioner drove with the other anonymous man at his side. The camphor, elm and cypress trees grew tall and wide along unfamiliar streets, providing shifting shadows.

The buildings we rode past were classically Chinese, with sloping, green-tiled roofs, and tiny parades of Chinese deities on the upturned eaves. There were no donkey carts and no bicycles. I guessed this must be where the high Communist Party officials lived and worked.

I was scared; and worse, no one knew this was happening to me. In Chinese, I asked the man sitting next to me where they were taking me. He remained silent, unblinking. *What could possibly be my crime?* I wondered. *Is it possible they have found out that Ming and I are lovers? Will we be paraded on the back of an army truck, denounced as enemies of the state, pelted with eggs and spittle, or even be killed?*

Our car was waved through a dark green metal gate that four Army guards quickly banged closed behind us. The driveway was made of crushed grey rocks; there were no trees, and the sunlight glinted harshly. Thirty feet later we stopped at a blocky one-story gray cement building. I wondered if the barrenness of this reception area was intentional, hinting a stark future ahead for anyone trapped in this capricious government's grasp.

The three men escorted me into a small, well-lit room. They sat me in a wooden chair at a green metal table. The chair's mate was on the opposite side. As they left, they loudly slid the lock in the door. Staring at me was an image of Chairman Mao, a smaller replica of the painting that overlooked Tian An Men Square, with the same puffy apple cheeks. A Chinese flag stood in the corner to my right. A small fan mounted in the other corner of the pale green walls swung in uninterrupted rhythm, moving air that remembered fear. A black fly buzzed.

I began to hear punctuations in the silence. The fan, as it clicked its reliable turn to the right, and the fat black fly making lazy, buzzy circles carved their effects in this noiseless room. Had I been forgotten? How would I know? The chair became harder the longer I sat. I needed the toilet. I wiggled on the chair some to try to settle down my bladder.

It seemed like hours later that a muscular woman officer entered the room and sat down crisply across from me. Before she could speak, I asked her if I was under arrest.

"Not exactly."

"Then why am I here? I want to speak to my embassy."

"I will ask you the questions," she boomed. "I will decide."

I jutted my jaw forward, underlining my demand to speak to my embassy.

She ignored my petition and flipped open a green notebook, pulling a pen from three in her breast pocket. Her demeanor softened. Her voice was lower, sultry in timbre as she asked me questions.

"Have you ever used chopsticks at lunch?"

"Sometimes."

She began writing.

"Have you ever been on a train?"

"Well, yeah." I fidgeted.

"Are you a student at the Language Institute?"

"Yes," I answered truthfully. "May I use the toilet?"

"You will wait."

She snapped the notebook closed and her piercing attitude

returned. She then stared at me for a long moment with one arched eyebrow that reminded me of a whip. She stood up and knocked her chair with the back of her leg. The chair skidded backwards on the rough cement floor. The noise, like swift racehorses, fractured the silence, startling me. I knew she had intended that little torment when she smiled sideways as she left.

Why would she ask these peculiar and off-center questions? Maybe they were questions full of traps with veiled trip wires, but how could I know? Was Ming worried I was late for lunch? Would I ever get out of here? I tried to talk myself into being brave but I was shrinking inside. I buried my head in my arms. I wanted to cry.

The small fan still stirred its hints and the black fly landed on the table. Maybe she was watching me through a secret hole in Mao's right eye. *Sit up straight,* I told myself; then she wouldn't know that the silence was getting to me. I folded my hands on the table but even though I tried to hold them still, they took on a life of their own. I started drumming, tapping a rhythm I had worked out for myself when I was five years old in a boarding school. A magical staccato that would keep me safe from the Catholic nuns after they found out I had wet the bed.

If I had to wait here any longer, I thought I'd start losing my mind, perhaps even seeing things that weren't really here. I had no way of telling time. There were no clocks, no windows to measure diminishing sunlight nor lengthening shadows.

When the starched woman returned, the black fly flew left, out the door. She put her hands heavily on the table. I looked at her, pleading with my eyes for her mercy. I wanted her to forgive some undefined transgression. Brushing aside my appeal, she leaned toward me, her jaw set forward, her black eyes piercing, and announced her decision.

"We will be watching for you. Do not return to the post office. You must stay away. If you go there again, we will arrest you for crimes against the People's Republic of China. You will be sentenced to many years of hard labor."

"I won't go there," I said in mumbled Chinese. I could smell myself sweating sour.

"Good. Now you can use the toilet, then I will drive you to the post office. You will get your bicycle and you will return to your institute."

She handed me some rough toilet paper at the bathroom door. There wasn't much privacy until I squatted down and felt unseen behind a two-foot high door. I felt instantly relieved, and wondered if this was a trick, if I might be put back into that room again. What did she mean when she told me I'd be watched? All the time, from then on, even at school? Forever?

I stood alone, exhausted, on the crushed rock driveway until a black car appeared. She opened the back door for me and indicated I should get in and then she drove me to the post office.

People gave me sideways glances as I got out of the car, some even whispered and pointed. Edgy, I kept my eyes down. I found my bike, and walked it to the road. When I swung my leg over the seat, I couldn't push the pedals; my legs were without cohesion, as if weedy strings had replaced my bones and muscle. But I had to get home to Ming; I needed the safety of her arms. I willed my legs to work and pushed the pedals hard.

I cursed my stupidity. I had inserted myself into a situation I knew nothing about and gone beyond Ming to get information as though I had an exception, an American exception.

Instead of going to my building, #8, I stopped at the men's building, #5, because there was a better chance that the telephone would be available. I called my friend Alice, whose husband was the Charge D'Affaires at the American embassy. She told me to lay low and to definitely stay away from any post office. I asked her what my crime was, that I had only gone to overhear conversations by way of checking out stamps.

"You have done nothing criminal, just idiotic. But right now, just the suggestion, even a hint, of being subversive will cause the Public Security Bureau to become circumspect and paranoid."

She assured me that the embassy would create a file on me so if I were arrested, her husband and the consular office would spring into action as soon as possible. She also told me to be careful about where I went. The Chinese government was overreaching and overreacting. Soon there would be a semblance of reason. I hoped she was right.

Now to Ming, oh god, what would she say? Had she been worried? She'd told me to stay away from Wang, that he might be trouble. I had ignored her warnings and his, seeking information at my peril, maybe our peril.

I opened her door. The smell of garlic whirled out and I breathed in deeply.

"At last you are here," she said. "I have been worried for you. We were going to have lunch together. It is almost five o'clock, did you forget?"

Remaining on the chopping block were a gnarled finger of ginger, green onions and even more garlic.

"Ming, something has happened. I may have made a terrible mistake."

Alarmed, she put down the cleaver. Wiping her hands, she took me into her arms and held me tightly as I sobbed.

Sitting down beside her on the bed, I fell onto her shoulder. She wrapped her left arm around me, just listening. I told her of going to the post office, being taken by the three men, and being driven to the secret part of town. I described the curious questions, and Alice's advice. I finished recounting the events by telling her about the officer warning me that I would be watched.

"You were very stupid to go there. You could be in prison now and no one would know how to find you. I told you I would tell you when I knew something."

"I know. I just wanted to find out more about the political

gossip. I was foolish. I am so sorry for causing you to worry."

I felt her body shift away slightly. Her arm slid down my back.

"No, please don't stop holding me. I need your arms around me to feel safe, so I can breathe again, until I can stop shaking inside."

Her shoulders slumped forward and she folded her hands in her lap. "When I was a Red Guard, I saw an old man beaten for reading a book of poems. He was blinded. I had to watch or they would have beaten me too. What you did reminded me that I could not help him, even to wipe the blood from his face, and it makes me afraid again." Her voice was powerful yet quiet. She stood up, shaking her finger at me. "Lu, you may have put our plans at risk now." She stamped her foot. "You are like the bull in a shop, an American bull. You are not special, Louise."

I felt fear again maneuver out from my belly and twist my skin.

"You must go from me now, I am too angry. I will come to you when I am ready to be with you again."

"Ming, I—"

"No more words. Just go," she yelled. "I will come to you."

I remained outside her door leaning against the chalky wall for a moment, as if just proximity would supply the comfort I drew from her.

I heard something slammed closed, the wardrobe drawer I guessed. I heard a muffled roar. I grimaced. I was the cause of this, her anger, and her fear. I reached for the doorknob and instead let my hand fall to my side. I walked to the stairs, glancing back once to see if she would open her door and come for me. She didn't.

Without turning on the light, I sat down at my desk and slumped my head on my arms. Tears dripped onto the cement floor. How long would she be angry with me? Had I done irreparable damage to us? I had been reckless. I couldn't undo this and I may have given breath to a creature that might one day consume us, a beast that could propel us into a horizon of fire.

I also considered whether there might be further danger to worry about. Would the secret police follow me everywhere I went? Did they just happen to be at the post office that day and investigate what a foreigner was doing there? Had they possibly been following me before? There was no way for me to know those answers. The secret police were shifty and disguised; they looked as in place as a bird feather on Tian An Men Square.

It was nearly eight o'clock when I turned on my small desk lamp. I was hungry. I got a bowl and poured hot water over some instant noodles. While I stirred the noodles, sprinkling in dried shrimps, I began to consider the tasks of contrition, consolation and restoration.

I needed to sleep.

The last thing I remember thinking as I lay in bed was that the same moonlight that poised itself on my hand also sought her.

A SECRET BOOKSTORE

和书店

I couldn't shake the officer's warning. Riding my bike to class and then to lunch, I found myself checking for unfamiliar faces, for spies maybe, or the secret police. And the disturbance I had created between Ming and me still lay heavy. When I returned to my room, I was sleepy. I lay down for a nap, planning to study after I woke up.

There was the sound of a key in a lock that I wove into my unsettled sleep. I awoke sitting straight up. Panic. *The secret police are here. That officer has come back for more.* Before I could scream, Ming wrapped me deep in her arms.

"It's just me. I am here. Everything is okay. *Shhh, shhh,* calm your heart."

I grabbed her and held on. Every string of fear, every thread of the beast poured out. Still she held me until the last gasps of terror and dread had been expressed.

"I am so deeply sorry for all of this. I wasn't thinking, of you or us. I . . ."

"I know you are sorry," she said hugging me tighter. "Promise me you will never go there again." For emphasis she tapped on my breastbone.

"I promise." I took her hand and waited for her to continue.

"I talked with Tian last night. I told her about you and the secret police. She said you are small potatoes. She thought the police just happened to be there and saw you and took you away to find out if you were causing trouble. Because they let you go, they have no more interest in you."

She sighed heavily and weaved our fingers together. "Tian also told me I was thinking only of myself. I was frightened and angry with you, but she was right. I put me first, but what you needed was bigger. For this I am sorry to you."

"If I had stayed away from the post office none of this would have happened. I am so sorry I did that. You know that, right?"

"I do. Yesterday I was afraid that I would lose you. Maybe you might disappear into a prison and I wouldn't be able to find you. To not have you with me made my heart cold."

"Did Tian have an opinion about whether I made us tall nails or not?"

She kissed me on my neck and said, "I asked her that, she said no because they let you go and they didn't come to me." She asked, "Do you want to get the radio today?"

"I do. Let's go."

Getting dressed and ready to ride into town, I was aware the tension that had been between us was lessening and I felt relieved and found breathing easier.

Turning south onto a less crowded road, I said, "I still don't understand why you don't like Wang." I coasted my bicycle a little closer to hers. "He seems nice enough, and well, like any teenager."

"He is a hooligan. Don't give me this trouble. You don't know about these things."

"Have you even met him?"

"There is no need to meet. He will bring trouble." Her words were sharp, so I let the conversation go and slowly widened the distance between our bicycles.

"After we buy the radio," Ming said, locking her bicycle, "You keep following me."

We entered the dragon-fronted double doors, and then walked through the tin toys department.

"There are things you should know," she said. "Even though I have told you about these things, I think you don't understand deep. You will see. Just do what I say."

We were in the biggest People's department store in Beijing, a full-block-wide and five-stories-tall shopping paradise. The two shopping areas near our school were strip malls compared to this, like the difference between a 7-11 and a Wal-Mart. The Communist government had provided and approved everything around us, and although most of the goods were of marginal quality, the store seemed to have triple everything, from enamel pots and plates to women's underwear festooned with peonies and butterflies to bicycle parts and carburetors.

I was buying the radio as a gift to myself for diligent study. My Chinese had reached a level where I had an increasing ability to appreciate *xiang sheng*, or "cross talk," a traditional oral Chinese comedy accented with puns and poetry, the Chinese equivalent of Abbott and Costello's "Who's On First?" routine. With the radio, I would improve all the more.

We stopped in the dry goods department where a wooden wall displayed several dozen bolts of colorful fabric. We leaned on a glass case full of rainbow-ordered embroidery and sewing threads, needles, thimbles and pins.

"Did you bring your ration coupons for the cotton?" Ming asked.

"Of course. Here." I handed them to her.

"I want you to come to me at this counter before we leave. Then we will choose some heavy cloth. I want to sew something for Ma."

Walking up the stairs to the second floor, I wondered what

she had in mind. "Why at that counter?" I asked.

"In case you get lost. I want you to see something by yourself."

The people descending the stairs stopped to gawk at me and caused a jam-up. I stood out in most of the places I went, and each time I understood a bit more what it meant to be "other," "foreign." I knew many of them had never seen anyone who wasn't Chinese before and that I was a novelty, but having people stare at me everywhere still sometimes made me grumpy. I harrumphed, ignored them, and followed Ming up the stairs.

The second floor held our first destination: radios. The air was lightly weighted with the scent of machine oil. Then I noticed there were saw blades, scores of wrenches and screwdrivers, motors, tractor and bicycle parts. I breathed in a familiar smell that offered a remembered comfort, that sweet scent of rust protection thinly applied to freshly cast metal parts. It had been a part of my work as an appliance repair-person at the Gas Company in Los Angeles. I picked up a disc blade wrapped in thick waxed paper and I remembered the promise of a pristine saw tooth.

Ming took my elbow and guided me to the radio department.

"You will do all the talking to the shop assistant."

"Just don't let me accidently ask for one of those tractor transmissions."

The shop assistant gave me her immediate attention, ignoring the shoppers she had been helping.

"What do you want?" she softly questioned.

"I want to buy an AM radio," I told her. "I want one that has good sound and doesn't cost too much. The best and least expensive."

I felt Ming at my hip and saw her encouraging me from the corner of my eye. I also became aware of a deepening circle of people pressing in on me, listening to me and watching what this "guest" might be buying. The shop assistant, noticing my discomfort, shooed the crowd away.

149

As she took three radios from the green glass shelf below our arms, she gave Ming a look that said: *why are you still here?* Ming shot back a sweet little *fuck you* look and then put her hand on my shoulder.

I chose the Spring Thunder radio and gave the worker the People's money, not the foreigner's cash, *wai hui*. I was a little delighted to see her disappointment, since I am sure she had imagined switching her People's money for the more valuable foreign certificates.

"Now we go to the third floor," Ming directed. "When I leave, you watch where I go. When I come out, you just walk in. Look quickly."

Again the flow of people coming down the stairs slowed to stare at me. It was easier to ignore them this time because I was intent on Ming's mysterious instructions.

"Ming, where the hell are you taking me?"

"Okay, we are close enough. I will leave you now."

I watched her go through a narrow door draped with a dark, heavy curtain and disappear. As I waited for her, I pretended to look at translucent rice-pattern teapots and cups. And when she reappeared, I casually walked through the same door.

It was a secret bookstore and I wanted every book I saw. There were tens of shelves and rows of pirated volumes: textbooks, fiction, nonfiction, reference books, and dictionaries. Every book in the world seemed available. I saw a book I had long wanted, *A Grammar of Spoken Chinese*. This cost more than one hundred dollars in America; here it was for just over a buck. I became lost in the availability of so many desired titles. I started to fill my arms with books like a child collecting cicadas in a bamboo cage. The shop assistant, who had been busy dusting shelves on the other side of this undisclosed area, hurried to me in a panic.

"Excuse me," he said. "You cannot buy books."

"Why?" I asked, cocking my head. "This is a bookstore for the people, right? I am one of the people. I can pay with *wai hui* or *ren min bi*. Which do you prefer?"

"They are not for sale to you, only for Chinese people," he said.

"Wait a minute here," I said in Chinese. "I want to buy these books."

He was politely panicking, and I wasn't going to let him off the hook so fast. I was certainly attracted by the cheap prices of the books and only slightly dismayed by the outright theft of copyrighted work. Obviously the government, in yet another enigma of life in China, had sanctioned this, since this was a government-owned store. I could see that he was just a low level employee because he had no pens in his pocket. The number of pens in a breast pocket was considered an unofficial signal of importance.

He was becoming more agitated. His eyes darted. The crowd in this secret section was gathering, watching the foreigner and the shop assistant in a verbal tussle. I backed down. I knew he was not responsible for this, so I just dumped my chosen treasures into his arms and walked out in an exaggerated huff.

Struggling through the always-gawking people down the stairs to the dry goods department, I found Ming waiting for me.

"Don't talk this yet," she whispered. "Wait for the outside."

I didn't want to wait. I was churning with questions. I started to mumble a "why?"

"No, outside only." She grabbed my wrist. "Now, do your job Lu, get the shopkeeper over here."

Using less Chinese than I knew, I beckoned the shop assistant.

Ming took over, asking the clerk to show her several bolts of cloth. As they talked and quibbled, I took advantage of the slight respite and calmed myself. She reminded the worker that she must be polite to the foreigner and give her the best quality. The worker cursed a little and took Ming's money and the ration coupons. I poked Ming in the ribs as the worker walked away with a bolt of thick, rust-colored cloth.

"You told her you were my cook?"

"I could have said I was your driver, but I don't know how to drive."

I rolled my eyes.

The shop assistant returned with Ming's bundle, placed her change, several aluminum coins, in her hand, and we left the store.

Approaching our bikes, me with my radio under my arm and Ming with her fabric, I could finally ask, "So, what's going on in that bookstore?"

"What you saw, you know."

"Where did those books come from?" I asked securing my radio on the back of my bike, as she put her package on the rack of her bike.

"I don't know, maybe from Hong Kong. It doesn't matter."

As I swung my right leg over my bike, I asked, "Why did you want me to go into that bookstore?"

"I decided that you needed to see for yourself that you are not special everywhere. You will not always have the privilege ordinary people give to you," she said as we paired up and began riding home. "You must remember this and be careful. We have our future to think."

"Do I act like I'm special or entitled?" I asked as we stopped at a traffic light.

"Sometimes, yes." She sighed. "Yesterday you went to the post office. I told you not to. That is what I mean. You think you know about things, but you do not."

We were on the move again. Her sentiment puzzled me. Did I consider myself privileged? I didn't think so; I tried to be conscious and courteous, but maybe what I knew wasn't enough. I was beginning to understand that I was just a guest and as such, I had an obligation not to poke my nose into things that were not my concern.

THROUGH A BACK DOOR

走后门

"Stop talking," she growled. "*Wo dao mei le.*"

Dammit, I thought to myself. *When she has her period she is irascible, her cramps are intensely painful, and she's cranky as an old steam boiler.*

She rose up on her elbow, and said, "*Peng zi. Quai.*"

I grabbed her washbasin and slid it under her chin just at the moment she heaved. Then she rolled into a ball, grabbed her lower stomach and moaned.

"*Wo shang si le,*" she said. "I want to die."

"I'll clean this, and be right back," I said. "Then I'll give you a hot cloth for your belly."

When I returned, she was standing on wobbly legs taking medicine that, hopefully, would relieve her pain. I noticed that she had also prepared six piles of neatly folded rags. I gave her a hot towel wrapped in a plastic bag and she fell into bed.

"How long until you feel better?"

"Maybe afternoon time."

"I will make you some tea if you'd like?"

Before she could answer, Elizabeth banged the door open.

153

"Lu. Ming. God fucking damn." She stopped in the doorway, her eyes careening, and her voice gravelly, loud.

"What?" I asked as I went to her.

Ming, in spite of her pain, rose up on her elbow.

"Guan has been arrested and put in jail," she bellowed, slamming her hands down on the desktop.

I stood there, not speaking, not breathing. Ming held herself upright for a few moments then sank back into the bed, her hands covering her mouth.

"Why, what happened?" I asked, closing the door and sitting on the chair next to her.

"Someone wrote an anti-government poster and put her name on it. The goddamn secret police came before dawn and took her away."

"Jesus, what are you going do?" I asked.

"I don't know, get a lawyer, go to the newspapers, I dunno, but I'm gonna do something."

We were all quiet for several minutes. Ming rolled over toward us. "No lawyers," she said. "Bribe."

"Bribe?" Elizabeth roared. "Who the bloody hell do we know to bribe?" Then looking at me, she said, "What's the matter with her anyway, she got the flu?"

"No, she'll feel better in a few hours," I said.

Elizabeth picked up a chair and set it down next to Ming's bed.

"What do you mean about bribes?" Elizabeth asked.

"I mean you or Lu can bribe a policeman and get her out," Ming said.

"How do I bribe a policeman? Are you out of your bloody mind? I could land in jail too."

"Tonight," she said pressing the warm cloth to her belly, "I'll talk to Tian. Her brother was in the Army police. He will know."

I looked at the clock on the desk. It was nearing four o'clock. We would have to wait until after five thirty when Tian came

154

home from work.

"I will come to Lu's room after I call to Tian. You two go away, your talking is hurting me."

"Let's go to the dining hall and talk," I suggested as we stepped outside Ming's room. "I'll just run up and get my meal tickets."

Putting the tickets in my pocket, I froze. I remembered that afternoon I had spent being detained and thought about Guan going through that same terrible experience. Recalling the dread and deep fear I felt then made my eyes swim, my pulse rise, and made me dizzy. I sat on a chair until my wits returned. Bribing the police seemed dangerous, and yet necessary. I felt familiar vibrations of fear in my bones. On impulse, I grabbed a sack of peanuts and went downstairs.

"C'mon buddy, let's walk. I don't know how we will pull this off, but by god we will make every effort."

We walked in silence; I had no words to offer and she seemed to need the silence to think through the events that had just happened.

The dining hall was, except for five or six scattered students, empty and quiet. We sat down at a table near the windows, away from the others. I poured some peanuts on the table and we both began to crack them open.

"Do you think she is alright?" Elizabeth asked, her bravado slightly diminished.

"I don't know. I sure as hell hope so." I didn't say that I was worried about her. Guan's health was delicate; she needed weekly medications to keep her bones strong.

"I'm starting to get worried, Lu. I have heard stories about women in Chinese jails. Rapes, beatings, the cells so cramped there is no room to even sit."

"Don't think about that stuff," I said, a little unnerved by the conditions she suggested but more, by her change in demeanor. Her confident, straight-ahead approach was frazzled.

Gathering the peanut shells then sliding them to a corner of the table, I said, "We have to start figuring this out. I know we are going to need money, probably a lot. How much do you have?"

"Right now I have 1000 *kuai*, maybe 700 in *ren min bi*."

"I've got 150 *ren min bi*, and 2,500 *kuai*, that gives us, right now, 3,500 *kuai* and 850 *ren min bi*."

"Why so much *kuai*?"

"Tuition is coming up. I've also got $300 US. That ought to be a boost."

"You know, of course, that I'll pay you back."

"I know you will," I said sweeping more shells into the corner. I was nervous to give her my money. If she didn't get it back to me on time I would have difficulty paying my tuition and that might mean I would have to leave Ming, my studies, and China sooner than planned.

"How did you find out Guan had been arrested?"

"Her roommate called me," Elizabeth said cracking five peanuts at once. "Two men and three women secret police came into their room, handcuffed her and took her away in a black car. Her friend asked a policeman why, and he told her about writing the subversive poster."

"Jeez, that's really serious."

"Her roommate also told me about an administrator in her department that had been jealous of Guan, kept trying to say Guan's published work was her own."

"Did you know about this?" I asked, squeezing a peanut loose from its red skin.

"Yeah. When Guan mentioned it, I wanted to rip the administrator's eyes out and chew her fingers off. Guan told her to do her own work, then ignored her and after a while she stopped trying to claim Guan's work, so she didn't give it another thought."

"You think it's her?"

"Her roommate thought so. Guan was decent to her, now maybe this fucking bitch has brought this on Guan." Elizabeth angrily flicked a shell across the table.

"Won't the police find out when they investigate?" I asked.

"They won't investigate. If you are arrested, you're as good as guilty. There is no rule of law in this bloody country. What time is it?"

"Just after five," I said. "Look, they just opened the windows for food, you want something?"

"Yeah, I haven't eaten all day."

When I returned to the table, Elizabeth was spinning a peanut with her right index finger, her face sagging onto her left hand. I placed two plates filled with what looked like a thin breaded patty of pork, a serving of fried potatoes, and a bigger serving of cabbage on the table.

"We'll get her out, try not to worry," I said setting her plate and fork in front of her.

We finished eating and Elizabeth bussed the dishes. I watched her walk across the expanse of the dining hall. Almost two years ago she had helped me when I was confused and overwhelmed. Now it was my turn to return the favor and I was glad for the opportunity.

She walked back to my room at a speedy pace; I trotted to keep up with her.

"Do you have any scotch?" she asked closing my door.

"The bottle you gave me is here somewhere. I'll find it for you."

Standing in front of my opened wardrobe, I wondered where I had put it. Elizabeth plugged in the hot plate and sat down.

"Here ya go," I said handing her the bottle. "But none for me."

Ming rushed into my room and sat down on the bed. We grabbed the desk chairs; Elizabeth put the scotch on the desk, and we sat down in front of her.

"Here is what we do," she began. "First, we need 3,600 *kuai* and five cartons of 555 cigarettes."

"Okay, good so far," Elizabeth said, nodding towards me. "I can get the money and the cigarettes."

"One carton is for the first policeman so he will let us see his boss. The boss policeman gets the money and three cartons of cigarettes. We have to open one carton and stuff the money in there."

"What's the fifth one for?" Elizabeth asked.

"The taxi driver."

"We have to be at the jail at two o'clock tomorrow. I must make the bribes because you two will make too much attention."

"Are you okay about doing this?" I asked Ming.

"I am afraid, and I don't want to. But I think Guan is more afraid, so I will just do it. I have to wear this pin on my jacket." She pulled out a vintage Mao button from her pocket, reminding us of another time of danger. "Tian's brother will fix this with the desk policeman so he will know why I am there. And 100 kuai is for Tian's brother. I get out of the taxi in front of the jail and go in. Then you give the driver the cigarettes and tell him to go to the back of the jail. After I bribe, I will come to the taxi. Then we wait for Guan to come out the back door."

We sat quietly, not looking at each other, unsure if we could really do this, unsure what would happen if events went badly. Ming was in the biggest jeopardy; we all knew it.

Elizabeth slapped her thighs, puffed out her cheeks, stood up and announced, "It's time for a whiskey." She found three red enameled tin cups and poured scotch into each, then passed them around. "When Guan is safe, we will celebrate. For now a toast to Ming."

We raised our cups and took a sip. It burned my mouth, Ming choked, and Elizabeth tossed it down with familiarity.

"I should be going," she said. "I need to buy the cigarettes and get the money together."

Opening my desk drawer, I handed her my 2,500 kuai and a hundred-dollar bill just in case.

After stuffing the money into her pocket, she said she would pick us up tomorrow at one o'clock, then she almost cried. "How can I, we, ever, ever thank you?" Ming went to her and took her by the shoulders. "You can't, so don't try. We are friends, this is enough."

After Elizabeth left, we rinsed the scotch out of the cups, and I kept Ming in the corner of my eye, aware of the weight she was bearing.

"You gave her your school money," she said, leaning on the desk.

"I did, and I am a little unsure," I said turning toward her. "If she can't pay me back on time, I will have to leave you and this school because I won't have the money for tuition."

"She will pay you." Coming to me and standing in front of me, she continued. "You gave her something very big, bigger than money."

We stood together for a few moments, our regard for each other deepening even more.

I took her hands. "When you offered to make the bribe you may have put your chance, our chance, to go to London together on the line." I waited a moment. "There is more to say, isn't there?"

"I am afraid my heart will change." She sat down on the edge of the bed. "Now I will tell you, this is very hard for me. A long time ago, in our village, there was a man that many respected. Because of our good thinking of him he became the leading cadre of our commune. A few years later he was different. He cursed people and no longer had compassion."

She sagged onto my shoulder. "Then we found out he was taking bribes and I saw how this had changed him. Now I have deep principles against this, I don't want to become him. Tian's brother also hates bribes. He did this for me and I did it for

159

Guan and Elizabeth. Now, like him. I will carry this stone for the rest of my life."

"If things go badly and we are caught," I said putting my arm around her, "we might have some protection from our embassies. You have no such sanctuary."

"I will do this because it is right. I will hope nothing goes wrong."

She took me into her arms and asked, "Will you just hold me tonight? My belly still hurts and I'm very tired."

She returned from the bathroom after placing a double amount of rags between her legs and we snuggled together until we found our comfortable fit.

Just before one o'clock the next day Elizabeth arrived with our taxi. I got in the back with her and Ming rode up front clutching the bag of bribes and gave the driver our destination. He looked at each of us in turn, furrowed his brow, and took off. Forty minutes later, nearing Heavenly Peace Boulevard, he suddenly pulled over.

"Why are you stopping?" Ming barked.

He mumbled something that I couldn't hear and shook his head.

"He won't drive to the jail, he's afraid of trouble," Ming translated.

"Drive you bastard, we're running out of time," Elizabeth yelled in Chinese.

"He will only take us to the Beijing Hotel, then we must get another taxi," Ming said.

"Bloody fucking coward," Elizabeth said in English.

Elizabeth boldly went down the line of taxis at the hotel, waving a fifty-kuai note, cajoling each successive driver. Finally, the fourth driver in line agreed to take us to the jail; if he drove fast we might not be late. I wanted to yell out to Guan to hold on, that we were coming for her.

Nearing the official section of Beijing, I looked at the clock on the dashboard: we were late. We grew quiet. Our jaws set tight. Finally, we stopped at the Beijing jail, almost fifteen minutes past two. Ming fingered the Mao button on her lapel, opened the car door and held me for a brief moment with her glance. When she disappeared into the station, Elizabeth told the driver to go around back and slipped him his carton of cigarettes.

We drove down a narrow, dark one-lane street. It was part of the old city: tight alleys with small homes, the intimate neighborhoods that the government was systematically destroying unless it suited other purposes, useful for jails and prisons.

The driver turned off the motor just beside a gray door, a gray that was darker than the tall brick wall it was set deep into. And we waited. Ten, then twenty minutes passed and nothing. Elizabeth had grabbed my hand a while ago, as much for comfort as for keeping herself inside the car. My knees began to quiver; I was afraid Ming might be arrested and I'd never see her again. Then a shadow passed quickly on our right side. Ming slid into the front seat and closed the door quietly. She said nothing, just stared straight ahead. I was so relieved she was safe I wanted to jump into the front seat with her. I bit my lip in small relief instead.

Another fifteen minutes passed and the driver leaned forward to start the car saying it was time to go. Ming scolded him, "Don't you dare. We wait." He snapped back into the seat. Ming grabbed her belly and I heard her wince, and still she continued to stare ahead.

A hinge creaked and yellow light wedged into the alley. As quickly as the light appeared, it was gone. Guan stood there, alone in the gray-dark light. I quickly opened the door and pulled her in; she fell onto our laps then slid into Elizabeth's arms. Ming yelled, "Drive. *Now*."

Guan whimpered and Elizabeth held her tight as we sped down the alleys and onto Heavenly Peace Boulevard.

161

"I can't see," Guan cried. "They broke my glasses."

The driver reduced his speed and asked where to go next. We hadn't thought of that. Ming took charge and told the driver to take us to Wu Dao Kou, then to take Elizabeth and Guan to the Friendship Hotel. When we got out at Wu Dao Kou, Elizabeth, holding Guan tightly, promised to call later.

We watched them drive off. Ming threaded her arm through mine and we began the short mile walk home. We didn't talk much, just let each step shed the anxieties and fears of the afternoon.

Closing the door of Ming's room we fell into each other's arms and began to cry, releasing the tensions that had clawed even deeper than we knew. Then we began to laugh and fell onto her bed laughing harder. We laughed at Elizabeth scolding the driver and getting the second taxi; we kissed each other strong and deep, gave comfort and tenderness. Taking a breath, we remembered that this was a hot water night and we could take showers.

"Let's go, I'll meet you here afterwards," I suggested.

"Yes, I need to change my cloths and clean myself."

Before she returned, the loudspeaker in the building announced my name telling me I had a phone call.

I raced down the hall and sure enough it was Elizabeth. Before we hung up, she promised to return my money by the weekend.

"Sweetcakes, Elizabeth called."

"How is Guan?" she asked as she stopped toweling her hair.

"She won't talk about it yet and she won't eat. She will stay with Elizabeth for as long as she needs."

"With time she will be good. Her spirit is strong."

I took up the towel and started drying the back of her hair. "I can't believe we actually carried that off, it was so dangerous. I was worried about you when we waited so long in the alley. That whole time I kept thinking the policewoman would show up

162

and we would all be arrested too."

I laid the towel down and pulled her closer. I took her hand and wove our fingers together. We both looked at our hands, the fit, so fine and true.

"Let's promise we'll always let each other know where we are going."

She agreed.

HURT

伤

It was just after six o'clock; I was deep into the second hour of learning my new idioms for the next day's assignment when I noticed that Ming hadn't come as she had promised.

I closed my books about seven thirty and went to her room. She wasn't there. The lights were off, the room cold. I snapped on the noisy fluorescent light and saw a note on her bed.

In a quick script she had written: *I will be back.*

There was nothing more, nothing about when she would return, where she had gone, or why. I sat down on her bed, and read her note several more times, as if more words would appear if I read it enough times. I sat there for a few minutes, feeling an inching fear, wondering if her disappearance was connected to the current political upheaval or my being detained. I wrote on the back of her note: *Come to me when you get home.*

I returned to my room, jumpy and worried. I paced. I sat on my bed. I sat in my chair. Although it was nearing eight o'clock, I decided to ride my bike to the Friendship Hotel just to bleed off some crazy worry. I wrote another note telling her that I was going to see Elizabeth and left it on my bed.

164

As I swung my leg over my bike, I remembered Wang's admonition: stay away from Qing Hua University, there might be danger. I turned left, avoiding the shortcut and possible risk, and took the long way to the Friendship Hotel.

I braked quickly at a newly installed, well-lit billboard. It showed photographs of dead people, their bodies severely mangled in traffic accidents. The text accompanying the photos blamed the dead people for polluting the streets with their guts and brains. Had this Spiritual Pollution movement really gone that far?

I pedaled hard to get to the hotel, needing to find Elizabeth; maybe she would know where Ming had gone and maybe there would also be other ex-pats, and we could compare notes on the threats of this political movement.

Five guards stood at the gate; usually there was one. They had me remove my white cotton mask and take off my brown fur hat. Seeing my blonde hair and round eyes, they let me pass.

I walked into the bar and saw a table of familiar faces. Elizabeth was there, as well as several acquaintances from England, Finland, and Yugoslavia. When they saw me, they waved me over to them.

They were hunched toward each other in uneasy conversation when I joined them at their table. Elizabeth immediately ordered a shot of scotch for me.

"Elizabeth, what the hell is going on?" I asked.

I took a sip of the single malt as Elizabeth cadenced a new slogan: "'Ignite the spirit of the masses to stamp out Spiritual Pollution.' People are being arrested for minor offenses," she explained. "It seems it isn't the crime; it's just the suspicion." She looked down to her glass cupped in both hands; her lips tightened. "I heard that in Harbin," she continued, "party officials arrested two men for being lovers, hung posters on their necks denouncing them, and then paraded them around town while their neighbors and friends were made to scorn them. Then they disappeared. There are rumors that in Zheng Zhou forty-five men were executed just for shoplifting."

"Oh jeez, I don't want to hear that," I said.

Elizabeth, sensing there was more to my arrival than camaraderie and gossip, put her hand on my arm.

"Can I see you outside for a sec?" she asked me. "We'll be right back," she said to the others.

We walked a short distance along a darkened portico, stopping near a moon gate.

"What is it mate?" she asked sitting down on a bench.

"Ming is missing." I could barely choke out my words.

I slumped onto the bench next to her and she put her arm around me. I told her about finding Ming's note on her bed. "What if she's been arrested or hurt and can't get home?"

"Try not to worry, Lu. She'll come back. If she doesn't return in a few days, we will help you find her."

"Days! I can't stand another minute. She always tells me where she's going. What the hell was she thinking, writing that little nothing note, that I would magically know?"

"It's not like her, I agree, Lu."

"She just can't be gone forever, can she?"

"Look, I'm just gonna ask this. Do you think this might have something to do with us bribing the police?"

We sat together in silence for a moment.

I rubbed my face with my hands. "Do you think they picked her up too? Oh god, what have we done?"

My shoulders heaved with fear.

Elizabeth, pulling me to her again, gave comfort. "She'll be back. Let's not worry yet."

I stood up, my anxiety reaching panic levels. "Elizabeth, I gotta go now and wait for her at home."

She hugged me tight. I promised her I would call if, or when, Ming got home, and bolted for my bike.

I got back to the Institute a bit after midnight. She wasn't in her room. I went to my room and saw that my note remained undisturbed. I crumpled onto my bed and slept in my clothes.

The third day was just like the first and the second, fraught with nausea, worry, and fear. She still hadn't come home. I went to class even though I was exhausted and gloomy and more, because there was nothing I could do but wait.

I checked for her bike on the way home, then stopped by her room. Nothing. She was still gone.

I slowly walked up the final steps to the third floor and saw Elizabeth standing near my door. I smiled at her, but she didn't smile back. A rope of panic seized my throat.

"Open the door, Lu."

I fumbled the key and dropped it. She picked up the key, opened the door and dragged me inside.

I grabbed her by both sleeves of her coat. "What? Why are you here? Tell me."

"Sit down," she said.

I couldn't sit down, I couldn't breathe. My mind was stirring lightning.

"Lu," she said, her face creased with concern. "Ming's been hurt."

"Oh god," I cried out, steadying myself against my desk. "Where is she? How bad? Tell me, dammit."

"She's in the Beijing #3 Hospital."

"What happened to her? Will she be okay?"

"Evidently a truck was trying to pass a donkey cart and bumped into her on the ring road just before dawn and knocked her off her bike. She has a long, deep gash on her right leg. There is a concern about infection."

"I'm going to her," I said, slapping the desktop. "Get a taxi for us now."

The pictures of the dead people on the billboard came to mind. I pushed them away; the thought that Ming's body could be on a billboard was unthinkable.

"You can't go, Lu."

"Oh yes I can, just watch me." I stood up and began searching for my keys. "I'm going with you in a taxi or on my bike right now," I roared.

"No, you can't, Lu."

She grabbed my arm.

I jerked it away.

"Get a grip, god dammit. Sit down."

I stood defiant, hands on my hips. I slowly collapsed as the realities began to sink in; I slumped down on the bed next to Elizabeth and melted into deep tears. She held me and handed me her handkerchief. My crying quieted some and I asked her how she knew Ming had been hurt.

"Remember her former lover, the doctor? She is attending to Ming. She knows about you, so she called Guan to get a message to you; she wanted you to know. Guan called me and here I am. She'll be here shortly with an update."

"I need to see her, Elizabeth, I really do."

"I know, but you can't and you know it. How would it look if her American lover waltzed in there and wailed all over her? Especially now in this political climate, do you want to put her in jeopardy too?" She grabbed my sleeve and twisted it hard. "There's just no way in hell you are going to her."

Guan knocked and entered; she hugged me, then Elizabeth. They sat down on the bed next to each other and I quickly slid the chair from the desk right in front of them.

"Her leg has a deep wound that needed many stitches," Guan began. "They change the bandages on her leg twice a day because so much blood comes through. Even though Chen gives her a calming drug, she keeps calling for you."

"Shit," Elizabeth barked.

"Chen tells the nurses she is just talking about the road," Guan said.

"Good for Chen," Elizabeth said. "Lu and *lu*, same words,

different tones, different meanings."

"Oh god, oh fucking god," I said, bending over, feral growls rumbling from my gut. "My dear, dear Ming."

"Chen will release her tomorrow afternoon about two o'clock. Then she will bring Ming here after her shift. Then once more to fix the bandage."

Elizabeth looked at me. "See mate, not so bad, she'll be home tomorrow."

"Elizabeth," Guan said. "You take Lu's meal tickets and go get food for us."

"Sure," she said. "But why don't we all go together?"

"Just you go."

I pointed to my desk drawer and Elizabeth took the tickets. I gathered up some pots for the food and handed them to her. After she left, Guan motioned for me to sit beside her on my bed.

I sat down and she took my hand. "When Ming comes home, there will be many who will want to see her: her friends, coworkers, the president of this Institute, and you."

I squirmed, not sure of what she was going to tell me next.

"I am telling you Chinese manners, Lu, and different manners for us, for gay people. When the others come you must not be here in the beginning. The people will come to honor their friendship with her, so you would interfere with the words from their hearts. You come later, say some words, and go quickly. This will be very hard for you."

"I'll want to hold her and be with her, you're saying I can't do that?"

"After the others are finished, you can go to her."

"I don't think I can do that."

"Then you must not go to her at all. You will embarrass her or cause danger."

I considered what she said. I knew she was right; we always had to be careful about what others saw, the impressions, the

169

inferences too quick to be jumped to. I wondered if I had the starch.

"I think I can do this." I paused, wondering if I really could. "I'll do it for her. She'll know I'm coming back later, right?"

"She will know. Trust her heart for you."

"How will I know when I can go to her?"

"One of us will come for you."

Elizabeth returned with dinner and as we ate, Guan told her about our conversation.

"These etiquettes are a bitch, right mate?"

"They fucking are." I swallowed a bite of potatoes. "Well, she'll be home tomorrow." I brightened a bit. "Then she'll get better and everything will be good again."

"Chen gave me this," Guan said pulling a folded plastic sheet from her satchel. "You put it on her bed just in case, so her blood won't go through."

"Yeah, Lu, you're gonna do it tonight while you clean her room. That'll give you something to do."

The next day, after class, I joined several classmates for lunch in the dining hall. I needed them to distract me from deeper worry. About 1:30 I returned to my room. At 2:00, I went to the first landing and leaned just right to look out of the window. From that angle, I could see arrivals at the front door. Finally, a taxi pulled up and a woman in a white coat hurried over to the other side of the car and helped Ming out. She was in pain; I could see that. Chen, I assumed, had Ming lean on her for support. Chen seemed caring as she helped Ming into the building. I listened to the commotion for more than an hour as folks came to help Ming or just to see her. I waited, gathering courage. I wilted and then washed my face. When Guan came to get me, I steeled my determination, took three deep breaths and went downstairs holding her hand.

When we entered there were two other people talking with her in hushed encouragement. Elizabeth was there, but I didn't dare look at her for fear my fragile courage would crack.

I wobbled to see her hurt. I wanted so much to gather her to me, to make her better, to ease her pain. Instead, I waited my turn. I sat on the edge of her bed. My voice lurched and my arms began to move to hold her. With mighty effort I caught myself, and said the common "get well soon" words, words that hopefully related my deeper heart to her. I could see in her eyes that she understood. I left as quietly as I had come.

In my room, I grabbed my bath towel, bunched it up and sobbed into it. I touched a blackness that was hot with incendiary landscapes. I didn't hear Elizabeth come in, but I felt her arm around me.

"Let 'er rip, mate, just cry it all out."

When I quieted, Guan had her arm around me too; I hadn't heard her come in either.

"Go wash your face, then go to her," Guan said. Patting my shoulder she added, "You did everything right."

I smiled at her, thankful for what she had taught me, and for being with me during this awful time.

"Go now," Guan said. "She has been waiting a long time for you."

Guan had lit two candles that flickered when I shut Ming's door. Her eyes were closed and I noticed the small bandage on her right cheek had been changed. I knelt down beside her and touched her golden face. She stirred and opened her eyes. We looked at each other for a long moment. She took my hand and held it in her two to her chest.

"Oh my dear, do you hurt much?"

"I do, but every day better. I missed you so much, Lu."

"I was so crazy when you were gone and even worse when I heard you were hurt," I said, tracing her eyebrow.

"Lu, lay next to me and hold me, I want your skin on me."

I tossed my clothing onto a nearby chair and slid slowly in next to her. I let her find her comfort next to me and I kissed her eyes. She was crying; I tasted her tears.

"Did I hurt you?"

"No, not too much. Chen gave me medicines, some for pain and to be calm," she said snuggling as close as she could. "Lu, hold me all night. I don't want to lose you."

"I'll hold you. I'll never let you go," I said wiping her tears. "We'll talk in the morning. Everything is okay now, we are together."

She whimpered.

"Just rest now, sweetcakes, I am here."

In the morning, I cleaned her chamber pot, gave her my vacuum bottle with hot water and my robe. Before I left for class, I kissed her goodbye and promised to bring a double lunch back for us to share.

When it wasn't my turn to write on the board or recite out loud, I drifted to unanswered questions. Where had she gone and why, and what was she doing riding her bike on the dangerous ring road at dawn?

I opened her door and was surprised to see her sitting at her desk. I bent to her and we shared a long-desired kiss.

"Are you feeling better?" I asked holding her hand, swinging it a bit. "I'm happy to see you. I was so damn worried."

"I am better." She smiled at me. "Chen told me to sit up for a while. Look," she said, standing slowly and turning. She opened the robe and I saw a gauze bandage wrapped around the length of her thigh. "It is clean. Chen said not too much worry for infections, but I still have to take the penicillin for many more days."

I helped her sit down and heard her wince for the final two inches. "Do you still have pain medicine?"

"I don't want it," she said settling as comfortably as she could into the chair. "I can't think with that medicine."

"I'll heat the lunch, you must be starved," I said, standing and plugging in the hot plate.

I set the vegetable pot on the edge of the hot plate and started to pick out a few pebbles from the rice. I felt her eyes on me. I turned to look at her. Her eyes offered a scale of pain I could not read. "Are you okay?"

"No," she said softly. "Lu, put a note on the door for no knocking."

"Okay, what is it?"

"Help me to the bed."

When she had settled, I wrote the note and locked the door. Just in case, I put a cup of water and her pain pills near the bed. I turned off the hot plate, sat down beside her and waited for her to find her words. I caressed her face.

She took my hand and said, "Lu, I went to my village. My sister called to me to come home fast. She was frightened."

"Why didn't you write that in the note? You didn't write anything useful, and it made me crazy."

"I don't know, I didn't think, I just went. I thought I would be back in the early morning. The bus is too slow, so I used my bicycle."

She turned her head away for a moment. When she looked at me again, she said, "I should have done better. I am very sorry for this, but my sister was crying hard and she told me Ma was crying too."

She squeezed my hand and said, "I know your heart, that you might think I left you forever, so Ma and I walked to the main commune building to call to you that night, but the phone was broken again. I left in the morning before dawn on my bike to come back to you."

"So that's what you were doing on the ring road."

"The truck driver who hit me drove away to find help. Two women stayed with me for a long time. Then a taxi came and took me to the hospital."

We were silent for a moment. I replayed the events between then and now.

"Why was Ma crying?"

Her chest heaved; with a growl like a tiger, she began to sob.

"Lu, now, come close to me."

Her urgency frightened me, and I lay down and edged closer to her. She moved herself fully next to me until she had her wounded leg over mine. She was crying; I could feel her leg heavy on me.

"I have very bad news for us," she finally began. "The Secret Police came to my village and talked to my mother; they told her they knew I was going to study in London." She squinched her eyes closed, her lips trembled; taking a breath through her nearly clenched teeth, she continued. "They told her that if I didn't return from London to Beijing they would put my sister in prison until I came back."

I seized. I could barely breathe. I had the lung-bursting sensation of a swimmer unable to reach the surface.

I had to say something just to get my breath going. "Would they really do that, just put her in prison if you don't come back?"

"Yes, they will."

"Why?"

"The government is afraid that all the smartest people will leave China forever."

I held her as tightly as I could, mindful of her wounded leg, afraid she might float away in this up-swelling political storm. We didn't talk. Unsettled, we held each other as we both softly cried. My thoughts began to drift to possible new designs, a search for an elixir of deliverance. And I deluded myself. *Things could change overnight for the better*, I thought, just as they had for the worse.

"We'll get through this you know," I finally said. "Somehow, we'll find a way."

"I'm afraid, Lu," she said, taking my hand to her chest. "The Secret Police came to my family."

"I know. That scares me too."

"What will we do now, Lu?"

"Right now, I really don't know. Our plans to go to America after London will have to change. Maybe we can only meet in London, then be together again here."

Fury began to lay tracks. I wanted to leap from the bed and break the chairs in the room and stick every splinter into the eyes of this barbaric government.

I didn't. I ate the bitterness.

A RENDING

一种读解

We had finished the written test of our vocabulary words, and I had successfully recited the paragraph I had had to learn by heart. Half listening to several classmates stumble and then recall their memorizations, I struggled to think of possible ways for Ming and me to be together. Hope is such a quiet little fuel. Maybe we could smuggle her onto a container ship to the States, or have her defect to the U.S. embassy in Beijing. Maybe even sneak her onto a train heading south to Hong Kong. But, what about her sister being imprisoned, who could live with that? No matter what I thought of, I knew it remained a delusion.

My teacher tapped me on my shoulder and told me that Teacher Su wanted to see me. I got up and started for the door when my teacher said, "Take your books with you."

This was an unusual request, Su usually met with his students in the afternoon after classes had been dismissed. Maybe, I thought, he wanted to know if I was still interested in the field trip to a duck farm he had been arranging.

"Please sit down, Lu," Su said, indicating a chair next to his desk. "Would you like some tea?"

"No, thank you."

"Lu, I have some news for you," he said sitting down at the desk. "Before I tell you, I want you to know that I did everything I could to prevent this."

Nervous, I pulled in my breath. I wrapped my kneecaps tightly with my hands.

"The Ministry of Education has given us orders to have all of our foreign students with college degrees from their home countries leave within three months."

He stopped talking and looked down to his pen, passing it from one hand to the other.

"This must be a mistake," I said. "Are you sure of this?"

"I am so sorry. I am sure."

He turned from me toward the window, saving face for both of us. I got up and walked into the hallway without breathing, every muscle tightening. Closing the door, I released the handle slowly and listened for the tumble of the cylinders finding their home. I stiffened again against the doorframe, my hands fisted. When I got to the stairs, I was wild. I could no longer restrain myself and took them two at a time, nearly stumbling, not seeing because my tears were thicker now. Outside, the cold, dry air stung my eyes. I didn't know what to do, where to go. I wanted Ming to fix it, to make everything right again. But she had gone to her village and wouldn't be back for hours.

I got on my bike and rode violently, fast, to the east. I was reckless to choose that direction; it's a perilous, two-lane stretch of road with an occasional stand of trees, exhaust-belching trucks, and choking yellow dust from the Gobi desert.

What would become of my dreams now, of Ming and our life together? Was my career gone too, based on capricious and unfathomable decisions by some old men?

I pulled over behind a thick tree, shielding myself from the traffic. I buried my face in my hands, too angry to cry. There were several large rocks at my feet. I picked up the first one and threw it hard, as far as I could, then another and another. I wailed like a wounded wolf.

Having exhausted my gritty-eyed fury some, I got on my bike and rode back. I weaved through the smoking mufflers, threaded my way through the congestion of grime and political conundrums. I went to find Elizabeth.

She opened her door after my first loud knock. Guan was right behind her.

"Your face is dirty," Elizabeth said taking my arm. "Lu, have you been crying?"

I flopped onto her sofa. They sat down on each side of me.

"Yes, goddammit, this fucking government is throwing out foreign students. That means me."

They looked at each other, then at me.

"Some of my physics students are having to leave too," Guan said. "I found out before lunchtime. I came right away to see Elizabeth, to talk this."

Nearly blubbering, I asked Elizabeth if she had to leave too.

"I had a meeting similar to Guan's. No, I don't have to go. This is only about students, not teachers. Jesus fucking Christ, what's next?"

"Does Ming know?" Guan asked.

"I don't think so. She went to her village two days ago to get ready to go to Oxford and start saying good-bye to Ma. She'll be back before dark."

"Something is burning," Guan said.

"Christ almighty, the sweet potatoes." Elizabeth pulled us both up from the sofa. "C'mon dammit, help me."

She banged open the oven door and the smoke became thicker. Grabbing the potatoes with a kitchen towel, she tossed them into the sink and turned on the water. Guan ran to the front door and opened it wide. We waved towels in the air until the smoke had mostly cleared and we began to laugh, gallows humor, laughing in the face of a death.

"Go wash you face, Lu. Then we'll have a scotch," Elizabeth said.

I looked at my face in the bathroom mirror and saw tear tracks down my coal-dusted face, my eyes red with grief and ire. Elizabeth was banging pots, slamming drawers, and swearing with a gusto and élan that only she could produce.

"What are we going to do, Elizabeth?" I said sitting down in a club chair. "What are Ming and I going to do?"

"I don't goddamn know," she said handing me a small scotch on the rocks.

"Let's think, Lu. There must be something we can do to outfox those bastards. Call your friends at the embassy, have them make you a worker instead of a student."

"I'd probably be assigned to some frozen outpost like Harbin. That won't work."

A wry smile began to make its way across Elizabeth's face. "We'll just bribe someone. We've done it before. Let me think. Guan, who do I know in the ministry of education?"

"Oh Elizabeth," I sighed, "that's just crazy."

"No, no, we can do this. We know people. We'll figure something out."

"You two," Guan said in Chinese, shaking her head. "I think you still don't understand China. Neither one of you are special. Just because you are Westerners doesn't mean that you can have everything only your way."

I remembered the secret bookstore Ming had taken me to. I understood what Guan meant about thinking we were exceptions.

"Delay the official papers," Guan said. "Do everything to the last minute. You can't stop it, but you can slow it."

"That's good, Guan. Makes sense," Elizabeth said.

"I guess that'd work for a while. But it doesn't take care of the long picture. I can't come back to Beijing and Ming and I won't be able to be together after her scholarship at Oxford ends."

"Ming," Elizabeth said. "This'll break her heart. This is one conversation I wouldn't want to have. How're you gonna tell her?"

"I guess I'll know what to say when I see her. God, I don't want to think about it."

"She must go to the USA with you," Guan said.

"Then her sister will be sent to prison," I said. "I don't think she'd manage in prison. She's not strong-spirited."

Guan stood up and turned away. Elizabeth and I looked down at our hands.

Guan turned around and snapped her arms to her side. "Ask her again, Lu. She will choose you. There is no better way."

I wanted her to be right, but any remaining hope was nearly gone.

"I'm going to ride home now, gather my wits, and figure out how to tell her. If you two think of another plan, a plan that will work, just give me a call."

Before Elizabeth opened her door she pulled me into a bear hug. I hugged her back and let her wonderful heart wash over mine. I savored her comfort. "Don't forget, my offer of airfare for you both is still on the table," she said kissing me on both cheeks. Then Guan hugged me tight as well.

Riding up to our building, I saw Ming's bike in the rack. I parked next to it and went straight to her room. She was putting fresh white eggs into her brown bowl.

"Ming." I flew to her open arms.

She held me and said in my ear, "I know. I met Su when I went to my office. We will find a way," she said taking my hand, as we sat down at the desk. "But there is more I have to say, Lu."

I studied her; we shared a shiver. I could see in her a slight shift, a breath held too long, an avoiding glance that paralleled my own.

"This has everything to do with Spiritual Pollution, doesn't it?" I said standing up from the chair. I wanted to hurl spears of

180

fire, sharp-edged rocks and little broken bottles at the ugly beasts that were heaving themselves between us. "I hate Deng Xiao Ping," I said slamming my hand on her desk. "I hate him. I don't think you or I have enough power to fight this. I don't think even the American ambassador can influence these politics. What are we going to do? What will happen to us now?"

"Lu," she said in a low, powerful voice. "Calm yourself. Sit with me, I want your hand."

Her request startled me. I looked at her and saw anguish. I sat down at the desk and she took my offered hand in her two.

"Lu, there is news worse than you know."

I watched as her face sagged. I watched her lips begin to tremble.

"Lu, I have lost my chance to go to Oxford. I can't go out to London."

My jaw slacked; there was a long exhale. I watched her tears river down her cheeks.

"My master teacher came and told me that Oxford University is withdrawing all invitations to Chinese students."

I thought for a second, and then asked, "Do you think this is their response to China throwing out the foreign students?"

"Yes, now I do."

"I don't know how but, by god, I'll find a way, some way, to make this work. There has to be something, some way for us to be together."

We sat quietly as the reality began to sink in, that this climate of political turmoil was beyond our influence, bludgeoning its way into our lives. How could we have been slammed into smithereens, skinned raw and left bloody in the span of a day?

I jumped up and pulled a growl from a place deep, deeper than I had ever known. She fell onto her bed, sobbing. I went to her. I lay on her back, trying to press the anguish from our lives. Her body shook as she cried. After a few long minutes, she rolled over and we grabbed each other, holding on with arms and legs at full muscle. We both cried without sound, the pain coming from a place too distant to have a voice.

"Just hold me, Lu. Make this all go away."

"I wish I could. I just don't know what to do."

We silently melted into each other.

She held me with incredible strength, so close that I could hear her heart breaking. Then she pushed me away.

TRAIN

火车

The next weeks moved to black. Nothing was easy. There was no place that didn't hold her color, her scent. Every taxi had trouble with its horn, every bike rider rode carelessly and the vegetables looked limp and rotting. The cicadas, once fascinating, now buzzed aggravation. Cinnabar faded to fish-scale pink, and gold no longer contained itself. Her color, her wild light, was oozing from my life. This anguish provided no angles to grab onto; the edges were shifty and elusive. This pain was patient and exacting. We often caught ourselves holding each other with our eyes, as if we were storing grain for the days of the deepest cold.

We fought. I chopped the broccoli pieces too large; she let the eggs burn in the frying pan. I lingered in the dining hall; she spent more time in her office. The frictions frayed us; we left murmurs and pleas unsaid. We began to shred each other over an asphalt of disappointments, of rages, and fears.

Still, there were times when we could be together with ease and laughter. We reminded each other of amusing moments, like the instance I called her mother an ignorant sunhat, and we laughed all over again. Sometimes our delight gave way to tears though, and Ming would plead with me to stay in Beijing.

"Please stop asking me to stay. You know I can't. I must be gone soon."

"I don't want you gone from me, Lu," she said in Chinese. "I can't bear the hole in my heart."

"Oh sweetcakes, c'mere," I said wrapping my arms around her. "My heart is breaking too. I so wish I could make this different, but I can't."

"I know, Lu. I know. Lie down with me now."

Holding her, breathing her in, I said, "Maybe in a few years the government will be different. If there is any change, I am coming to get you."

"We will write many letters. If the change comes, I will tell you. Then we will have white hair together."

I decided I would leave as soon as I could. I stopped going to my classes and began sorting through my books, pots, pans, and clothing, choosing what to take, to sell, or give away. Without her, there was nothing left for me in Beijing. When I told Ming about my decision she turned away from me.

"I want you to stay with me, don't go from me too soon."

At noon, on my last full day, Ming and I decided to walk to the village to buy the stuff of dinner. We needed pork, lacey cabbage, and apples. She wanted to cook *zhao zi* and honey apples, two of our favorite dishes. We passed through the west gate, stepping over the ubiquitous steel pipe. A light gust of wind lifted a discarded oil ration coupon. I picked it up and handed it to her.

"I've changed my mind. How about we get something quick and then come home?"

"No," she said. "I want us to cook together one more time."

"But I don't want to cook." I was becoming annoyed with her again. "I'm too tired and sad to do that. Let's just get some dumplings and be done with it."

"No." She was irritated. "If you want dumplings, I will make them."

She stopped, and looked into my eyes. I could read her intention of a truce, no more fighting or misplaced anger. Our time was too short; we both knew it. I smiled and nodded, signaling my agreement.

We walked slowly, occasionally squeezing each other's hand. Brown dust puffed over our shoes. The street bustled with wooden carts loaded high with coal cakes, pulled by donkeys that strained under their burdens. There were bicycles impossibly loaded with sofas, or tables and chairs, and on others, whole families of four. When she leaned into me, the edges of my pain crackled.

As we got closer to the shops, I could smell that glorious waft of frying sesame oil, pork and onion: *shar bing*. She had taught me how to make these fried wonders, and this would be one of the skills I would bring back to America. I wondered what lay ahead for me in the States. I'd need a job right away, and to find a place to live, but those tasks seemed fraught and Herculean. I looked forward to seeing my old friends, but not much more.

I thanked the fry cook and handed Ming a *shar bing*, wrapped in *The People's Daily*, the oil fittingly staining the name of Deng Xiao Ping. We found a bench under a camphor tree, leaned forward to keep the oil off our shoes, and crunched. We scuffed the soles of our shoes on the camphor leaves and remembered that fragrance, like dried rosemary leaves, from the day of our first kiss.

We looked at each other and laughed softly. Each of us remembering the day we went to the Ruins of the Summer Palace. It seemed to be ten thousand years ago, both of us knowing how far our friendship, our love, had come since that day.

For the last time, I did my job as the "foreigner," and received a slab of pork, pink, without too much fat. We moved on to the vegetable and fruit sellers and I was given the freshest cabbage and then the finest apples.

Back in her room, I began to chop and pound the pork; she started to prepare the cabbage and I heard her begin softly crying. I put down the cleaver and wiped my hands. I knew we weren't going to eat that night.

"Lu, I can't be with you when the taxi comes to take you away," she said pulling me in close to her. "Tian, Elizabeth and Guan will be there for you, but I can't bear to see that. I will leave in the morning at dawn and go to Ma."

"You are probably right not to see me off. I am not sure I could endure your tears and mine too. But I want to have every last minute of you."

Guiding her to the bed, I slowly removed her clothes, softly kissing each newly uncovered spot. When we were naked, I lay down and pulled her to me.

Our lovemaking was languid and tender, as if memorizing the tiniest tract of skin, or receiving the faintest quiver to a fingertip, would remain reachable in a time of unmanageable need.

Stroking my hair, tracing my nipples, placing her sweet little kisses on my face, the kisses that occur in the intimacy of being spent, she whispered, "I will miss the way your voice fills my heart. You do love me with your deepest heart and you didn't fall into pieces. I think you finally know that I do love you."

She rolled herself fully onto me. I could smell her hair. Feel her weight. I took in her breath. She laced her fingers through my hair, each of us holding tight with legs and bones, fingers and arms.

"I will never really leave you, Ming," I whispered in her ear. "I will always live in your heart. And you will live forever in mine, and in my deepest extra heart too. And even though this is the hardest thing I've ever done, I don't regret a single day or

186

moment of loving you."

Resignation and profound sadness pressed our bodies. With a murmur of defiance, we fell asleep holding our fit.

At first light, Ming prepared to leave for her village. She wrapped up the food to give to Tian. We kissed each other for the last time with tears rolling down our cheeks; our trembling, slippery lips barely worked. I stood for a moment looking at the door she had just closed behind her and wrapped my arms around myself and wept.

From her window, I waited for her to appear and then watched her ride slowly away. Her shoulders heaved. I reached for her through the glass, wanting just one last touch. I turned away from the window, I pressed in my mind the images of our simple life: the hot plate, the brown bowl, the chopping board, and her bed. This concrete floor, this blue-chalked walled room that contained the meals we prepared, sometimes feasts, sometimes fights, and our loving and lovemaking; all this and more had dusted a golden patina on every surface. The purple hyacinth, in a slice of wild mauve morning light, was the last thing I saw.

I closed her door for the last time.

Back in my now bare room, I sat on my desk chair. Alone. With my eye, I traced the cracks in the cement floor, following those veins to the empty bookshelf, the bamboo drying rack, and the windows looking out into treetops. I would miss this tiny spartan room, my studies, my friends, and her.

My two suitcases, packed, stood by the door. The food for Tian sat on my bare desktop. I had stripped the bed, rolled up the pad, and used a wooden box that held kitchen items, towels, curtains, and books that were for whomever wanted them, to hold the pad in place.

Elizabeth and Guan arrived with a taxi to take me to the train station and helped me carry my suitcases downstairs. Several classmates stood next to the taxi to say goodbye. Teacher

187

Su had also arrived, and my favorite grammar teacher came too. She thanked me for making her laugh with my earnest mistakes. I almost couldn't hear her; my heart was fleeing the ache of already missing so much.

I found Tian last and gave her the bundle of food. She kissed my wet cheeks, and handed me a small white box.

"This is your lunch for the train trip," she said in Chinese.

Once the taxi was loaded, I sat next to Elizabeth in the back. Guan sat next to the cabbie and he began to drive slowly away. I wanted him to hurry so I could speed through the agony, just to find some ease, just a little.

"You must be a good friend," he said in Chinese. "There were so many people to see you leave just now."

I couldn't talk. If even one word had broken free, I would have become undone. I could only nod. He quieted when Guan touched his arm.

Elizabeth handed me an envelope.

"What is this?"

"It's a round trip ticket. I am inviting you to Australia, spend some time with me at the ranch."

"Your ranch? How can I..."

"Don't thank me, goddammit. Christ almighty, I'm gonna blubber."

I thanked her anyway and folded the envelope and put it in my pocket. Right then I was nearly sure I would be sending it back to her. She looked away and blew her nose. Then she took my hand and I leaned my head on the window, watching the city of my deepest love recede. I saw mounds of watermelons stacked next to the abundance of cabbages. Some of the men wore magenta tank tops that strikingly revealed their muscles; others wore a deep aqua blue. I rolled down the taxi window an inch or so. I could hear the jumble and havoc of bicycle bells, car horns, peasant men urging their donkeys forward, and the cicadas.

At the train station, while I paid for my one-way ticket to Hong Kong, Elizabeth and Guan sat on a sofa in the first-class area waiting for me. Ticket in hand, I sat down between them.

We just sat there silently, together. We watched the country folks attempting to use an escalator for the first time. We smiled at the brave ones who completed the journey, and nearly clapped for their success.

"Being back in the States is gonna be rough, mate."

"I think so. I don't really know how I'll manage without Ming. It's just so damn hard. I hope to spend some time with my friends and get used to being an American again. But, you know."

"I do, mate. Let's make sure we write to each other. And Guan and I will take care of Ming for ya."

"Promise?"

"You got it."

The public address system announced that my train was boarding, and our shoulders sagged in unison. We stood up, then hesitated, not wanting this farewell. After a few moments, we hugged strong and kissed wet cheeks goodbye.

"See you at my ranch dear mate," Elizabeth said at last. "Cuppla months, okay?"

I waved as I walked, alone, down the buffed cement walkway.

The porters had already loaded my suitcases into my first-class compartment. Although I preferred to travel third class with the people, this time I was carrying a broken heart and I needed more room. I sat on the sofa bed, thinking of nothing, looking at the lace curtains, the red thermos and the packets of jasmine tea. The train lurched forward and jolted me to the truth that I really was leaving. I wanted to run from the train back to her, I didn't want to leave her. I still wanted to provide the essentials of her heartbeats. I reminded myself that I would never be able to give this gift to her again. I remained slumped on the sofa, quietly crying, as the train picked up speed and hit

189

its stride.

Hours later I opened the lunch box and next to an apple was tucked a small scroll. I knew that Ming had managed to put it there. Undoing the thin red ribbon, I let it fall to its full length. I recognized the style, it was written by the most skilled calligrapher in Beijing.

For your remembrance, it read, *Beijing 1983*. And last, my name, *Lin Xiao Min*.

A small but long piece of rice paper fell from the scroll. Ming had written in her own calligraphy a line of poetry from the Qing dynasty:

"When the water and sky become one."

ACKNOWLEDGMENTS

First, and where my deeper thanks belong, is to Terry Wolverton. Oftentimes in life we are graced to meet a true teacher and she is this beyond measure. Her support and guidance have been superior. When I first began writing this book, I doubted that I could gain sufficient skills to do the story justice. "I believe in you," she said.

And great cheers to my fellow workshoppers at Writers@ Work. All of you, from when the book was born to the present, have had an influence on my work and my growth as a person.

My deep gratitude recognizes Donna Frazier Glynn for her unerring guidance, and Alice Bloch whose influence with this book saved me from egregious errors.

And I salute Rachel Blakey and Kat Bormann for their support through Covid-19 and more, so much more.

To all my friends who were there for me, to kick my butt, lend a shoulder, or offer soft applause, thank you.

Thank you to Katherine Forrest for passing my manuscript on to Bywater Books, to Salem West for saying yes, and to Fay Jacobs for delightful content editing sessions.

With my whole and extra heart, I sing horizons of gratitude to Ming.

Read on for an exclusive excerpt
from *Light Is to Darkness*, the compelling sequel to
The Language of Light.

LIGHT IS TO DARKNESS

by Kathleen Brady

Coming from Bywater Books in 2023

UNBREAKABLE

牢不可破

Los Angeles was beginning to billow and flutter in pastels. The city was just days away from the start of the 1984 Olympic games. Everyone I knew was anticipating the competition with great excitement. There were also logistics to consider, how to handle the tens of thousands of out-of-town visitors and their impact on the freeways. The mayor had ordered delivery trucks to work through the deep of night and stop at dawn. Many locals were concerned that that wouldn't be enough relief so they left town. The result was heavenly. The freeways moved swiftly, pollution was reduced, and the treasured plein air of late summers in LA was especially celebrated.

I, however, was slate black flat. Since returning from Beijing, my despair was steep and so considerably wide that my will to reintegrate to an American life and join with my friends was nearly nonexistent. There was food in the house thanks to my friend, Theresa. My friends were concerned about my lack of participation in events and outings they arranged, they did keep a good eye on me. I would come around. I knew it, and they trusted me, that I would not let them or myself down.

Everywhere I missed Ming; there wasn't a single time or place when I wasn't wounded by her absence.

I was eating a saltine when the phone rang.

"Is this Louise McLean?"

The voice was deep, weathered, and unfamiliar.

"Yes?"

"Do you know a woman named Ming?"

I paused, unsure and beginning to spin.

"Maybe. Why? Who is this?"

"I am a Consular Assistant for the US embassy. This woman has defected from the People's Republic of China by way of their women's basketball team. She says she knows you."

"Yes, I do know her." I stopped breathing for a moment.

"How did you get this number?" I asked.

"I called the number Miss Ming gave me. A woman named Mrs. Healy gave me your number. Come to the Federal Building on Wilshire in West LA. There are details you should know. What kind of car will you be driving?"

"A VW Rabbit. Silver. Anything else?"

"Ask for Officer Ryan at the underground parking garage, they will allow you to enter. Your code word is 'buttermilk.' Use this with the lobby security, they will tell you where to go next."

"Tell her I'm on my way." But he had already hung up.

I showered, got dressed and was out the door in about ten minutes. I thanked myself for giving Ming Eloise's phone number before I left China. And a silent bigger thanks to Eloise's father for lending me his extra car.

I decided to travel on Wilshire Boulevard. From my small apartment in Echo Park it wasn't the fastest way to the West Side, but it was straight and I could gather myself before I got there.

So many questions peppered my mind. She wasn't particularly sports-minded, so what was she doing with the basketball team? How did she decide to defect? She would stay with me of course, but what would happen in a few weeks from now, or months? Did we still have what it would take to be together for years to come?

Accelerating through a yellow light at Fairfax Avenue, I was glad I had vacuumed and changed the sheets yesterday. Even though Eloise now had a hint, I looked forward to my friends' surprise when I could tell them Ming is actually here. I began to consider the possibility of danger. Would Ming be safe with me? Would I be safe as well? What would we do, where would we go to avoid harm?

Reaching La Cienega, I wished I had chosen to drive on Olympic; I wanted more speed now. I was settling from the initial news and wanted to get to her as fast as I could. I had been back in the States since the end of February; it had been five months since we had seen each other. I reminded myself of the manners, Guan, my friend in Beijing, had taught me: don't go running to her and kiss her all over. Keep it subtle.

Driving through Beverly Hills, passing Rodeo Drive, I smiled. The contrast of my old Chinese life and this wealthy shopping street nudged me a little more into my remembered American familiar.

As the Federal Building came into view and I approached the parking entrance, I asked for Officer Ryan. The guard instructed me to park on sub-level 4. Down like a drain I swirled. Occasionally I straightened the wheels a bit, but otherwise I held the steering wheel in the full left position. The parking area was, save two cars, empty. I parked, headed for the elevator and touched "M." I arrived at a sterile, wide-open lobby with guards stationed at two turnstiles.

"Your business?" the shorter guard asked.

"Buttermilk." I guessed this was the time to use the code.

The guard released the turnstile and motioned me forward.

"Take the left elevator to the 7th floor," he directed. "You will be met there."

The elevator doors slid open onto an empty hallway. I stepped out and looked both ways wondering where I should go next. Halfway down the hall on my right a door opened and a tall man with bushy silver hair and moustache beckoned me with three fingers. As I approached him, he offered his hand and introduced himself as Officer Ryan.

"This way," he said and we walked into his office.

Sitting near a window, looking small and fragile, was Ming.

I wanted to run to her and scoop her up and kiss her and hold her. She gave a discreet gesture of *no,* and came close enough to me to just shake hands. I understood her.

Ming and I sat down in leather office chairs in front of his desk.

"Now your friend is here so I will tell you both what will happen next. You will fill in Form I-589; this is an application for asylum and for withholding of removal. Remember exactly what you write because you will be asked about this when you have your hearing. Any questions? I have less than five more minutes."

"When does she have to return this form?" I asked.

"She has one year. If she is late," looking directly at Ming, "there is no grace."

"Is she in any danger from the PRC?"

"It's possible," he said. "I or someone will call you and use your code if we hear of any developments in that area."

"Should we get a lawyer?" I asked.

"I would advise that you do. My apologies, I have another appointment," he answered. "Miss Ming, you are free to go with your friend."

We three stood up in unison; he walked over to the door, opened it, and as soon as Ming and I stepped into the hallway, he shut the door.

Ming melted into my arms. She was shaking, but not crying.

"Let's go," I said. "I'll take you home."

She nodded and without talking, held my hand tightly all the way down to the car.

As I unlocked the passenger side door, she said, "Oh Lu, hold me strong now."

I held her and after a few moments her shaking began to slow. Hugging her was beginning to feel wonderful. I breathed in her sweet scent, taking me back to our simpler times in Beijing. It had been long months since we fit ourselves together. We began to be happy to see each other.

As I drove, she realized that she couldn't hold my hand because my car had a manual transmission, so she just held onto my forearm. I kept my hand on the gearshift knob.

I knew not to ask about deeper subjects, like how this would affect her family, until she brought it up, so I made small talk.

"Are you hungry?" I asked. "Want to stop and get some food to go?"

She just shook her head.

"I have eggs at home, would you like that?"

"Yes, your home."

Turning left onto La Brea from Olympic, I felt a deep fatigue begin to creep like a heavy fog. I sighed loudly, surprising myself and startling Ming.

"Are you tired, Lu?" She turned slightly toward me in her seat; she dropped her hand from my arm.

"Yes, I think I am. It's been quite a morning. But I bet you're even more tired?"

"I am," she said in Chinese. "Very tired. I have been awake since one o'clock yesterday morning when I ran away from the hotel."

"We can take a nap when we get home, if you'd like," I said turning right onto Sunset. "Whatever you need."

"My body is very tired, but seeing this city is very exciting. I want to see everything."

"We can do little tours of the sights of LA, and eat many

different foods, but they'll have to be cheap. I just have a part-time job at the newspaper working in the Opinion Poll. It's irregular work so we'll have to be careful of money."

"Ma gave me some money, but it is still in *wai hui*, so I must change it."

"There is a money exchange in the Galleria, we'll do that later."

"I wish it was more because maybe I come like a stone into your life," she said. "I know I am a surprise for you."

"Not a stone, for sure, just an adjustment for both of us."

Four hours ago I had been in despair, trying to manage my grief and now, like some kind of miracle or a ride on a dragon's breath, she was here. Unexpectedly the gears and levers of my life were changing; in fact, they were changing for both of us.

I occasionally glanced her way as she took in the sights of her new city. She looked, in spite of being exhausted, thrilled by everything we drove by. The huge mechanical billboards on the Sunset Strip blasting their "buy this and you'll be happy" messages had her chin on her chest. Driving past Grauman's Chinese Theater, she pointed excitedly and said she'd read about the movie house in tourist guides. Experiencing her excitement with everything so new to her was great fun. And there was so much more ahead for her. For us.

Nearing the apartment, I began searching for a parking space. I found a spot about a block away that just barely had enough room to fit my little car.

"Welcome home," I said unlocking my door. My apartment was one almost-large room, with a separate kitchen and bath.

She walked in and admired the carpet and the queen-size bed Wendy had lent me. She walked over and looked out of every window, then at the sparse furniture. "Lu," she said in Chinese, "I think an Empress must live here."

We both laughed. Compared to the rooms we had in Beijing, my place certainly was a palace.

Then she stood in the middle of the room and covered her face with her hands; she began to melt.

I rushed to her and took her close, held her strong.

"Oh, Lu," she said. "So much to talk. I am so tired."

"Let's lie down on the bed and we can talk."

"I want your skin on me, Lu," she said.

As she removed her clothing, I pulled the covers down on the bed. I was right with her as we fell together onto the bed.

That long desired touch of our bodies was at once transcendent. We savored each other, breathing out in unison our deep pleasure of reunion.

Our lovemaking was initially wild, as though we had to hurry to fill each other up. When we caught our breath, we slowed and caressed, and our kisses became tender.

I traced her eyebrow with my finger. She smiled. We held each other with our legs and hips.

"The last time I saw you, you were riding your bike home to your village. I saw you crying and reached for you through the window, wanting just one last touch. Until today, I thought we would never be together again."

"I cried for you all the way to my village," she said. "When I got home, Ma made me eat noodles, then she sat by my side while I cried and slept for many days. Anytime I was awake, I tried to imagine where you were. I didn't know, but I could feel the distance growing far."

"How did you make this happen?" I asked.

"A friend from college is an athlete. She is also a helper coach for the women's basketball team. When they knew they were going to the Olympics she remembered me and asked me to be a translator for the team."

She kissed my hand for a moment then continued. "I saw my chance to leave Beijing and come to you. I was worried for many things. But biggest I was afraid of the Chinese government catching me."

She was correct to fear how brutal the PRC could be. Being sent down to the countryside nowadays was more like a relaxing vacation, compared to the reeducation that was now spent in a heartless prison for an indeterminate length.

"Did your friend know what you intended to do?"

"No," she answered. "Just Ma."

Right then I wanted to ask about Ma and her sister; I was concerned for their well-being. I reminded myself to wait until Ming was ready.

"You are so brave, and that you did this is amazing. How did you know what to do?" I asked.

"I borrowed American travel books from my British students. All of the books had sections about laws."

She closed her eyes and held my hand in her two. "Lu," she said, opening her eyes, fixing with mine. "Do you still want me?"

"Oh my dearest you," I said. "More than the ocean wants the sky. Yes."

She rolled on top of me as I pulled her closer. We held that embrace for a long moment.

"We can do this now," I said. "We can have forever."

ABOUT THE AUTHOR

Kathleen Brady is a native Californian, though she spent three years living in Beijing, China. Her career has been varied, including stints in clinical psychology, journalism, healthcare, and various and sundry blue-collar jobs. As an author, she has published several freelance pieces in the *Los Angeles Times*. One of her short stories earned Honorable Mention in the Glimmer Train Short Story Awards for New Writers. Kathleen has studied writing with poet Eloise Klein Healy and award-wining author Alice Bloch. She continues to workshop with novelist, memoirist, poet, and editor, Terry Wolverton.

A graduate of Immaculate Heart College, Kathleen currently lives and writes in Los Angeles.

At Bywater, we love good books by and about women, just like you do. And we're committed to bringing the best of contemporary literature to an expanding community of readers. Our editorial team is dedicated to finding and developing outstanding writers who create books you won't want to put down.

For more information about Bywater Books, our authors, and our titles, please visit our website.

www.bywaterbooks.com

CPSIA information can be obtained
at www.ICGtesting.com
Printed in the USA
JSHW020904061221
21005JS00001B/1